Agatha Christie

Poirot
Investigates

HARPER

HARPER

An imprint of HarperCollins*Publishers*
77–85 Fulham Palace Road,
Hammersmith, London W6 8JB
www.harpercollins.co.uk

This *Agatha Christie Signature Edition* published 2001
1

First published in Great Britain by
The Bodley Head Ltd 1924 and Triad Grafton 1983

Copyright © 1924 Agatha Christie Limited
(a Chorion company). All rights reserved.
www.agathachristie.com

ISBN-13 978-0-00-793699-1

Typeset by Palimpsest Book Production Limited,
Grangemouth, Stirlingshire

Printed and bound in Great Britain by
Clays Ltd, St Ives plc

Contents

1 The Adventure of 'The Western Star'   7

2 The Tragedy at Marsdon Manor   43

3 The Adventure of the Cheap Flat   65

4 The Mystery of Hunter's Lodge   89

5 The Million Dollar Bond Robbery   111

6 The Adventure of the Egyptian Tomb   127

7 The Jewel Robbery at the Grand Metropolitan   151

8 The Kidnapped Prime Minister   177

9 The Disappearance of Mr Davenheim   209

10 The Adventure of the Italian Nobleman   233

11 The Case of the Missing Will   251

Part 1

The Adventure of 'The Western Star'

I was standing at the window of Poirot's rooms looking out idly on the street below.

'That's queer,' I ejaculated suddenly beneath my breath.

'What is, *mon ami*?' asked Poirot placidly, from the depths of his comfortable chair.

'Deduce, Poirot, from the following facts! Here is a young lady, richly dressed – fashionable hat, magnificent furs. She is coming along slowly, looking up at the houses as she goes. Unknown to her, she is being shadowed by three men and a middle-aged woman. They have just been joined by an errand boy who points after the girl, gesticulating as he does so. What drama is this being played? Is the girl a crook, and are the shadows detectives preparing to arrest her? Or are *they* the scoundrels, and are they plotting to attack an innocent victim? What does the great detective say?'

'The great detective, *mon ami*, chooses, as ever, the simplest course. He rises to see for himself.' And my friend joined me at the window.

In a minute he gave vent to an amused chuckle.

'As usual, your facts are tinged with your incurable romanticism. This is Miss Mary Marvell, the film star. She is being followed by a bevy of admirers who have recognized her. And, *en passant*, my dear Hastings, she is quite aware of the fact!'

I laughed.

'So all is explained! But you get no marks for that, Poirot. It was a mere matter of recognition.'

'*En vérité!* And how many times have you seen Mary Marvell on the screen, *mon cher*?'

I thought.

'About a dozen times perhaps.'

'And I – once! Yet *I* recognize her, and *you* do not.'

'She looks so different,' I replied rather feebly.

'Ah! *Sacré!*' cried Poirot. 'Is it that you expect her to promenade herself in the streets of London in a cowboy hat, or with bare feet, and a bunch of curls, as an Irish colleen? Always with you it is the non-essentials! Remember the case of the dancer, Valerie Saintclair.'

I shrugged my shoulders, slightly annoyed.

'But console yourself, *mon ami*,' said Poirot, calming

Poirot Investigates

Agatha Christie is known throughout the world as the Queen of Crime. Her books have sold over a billion copies in English with another billion in 100 foreign countries. She is the most widely published author of all time and in any language, outsold only by the Bible and Shakespeare. She is the author of 80 crime novels and short story collections, 19 plays, and six novels written under the name of Mary Westmacott.

Agatha Christie's first novel, *The Mysterious Affair at Styles*, was written towards the end of the First World War, in which she served as a VAD. In it she created Hercule Poirot, the little Belgian detective who was destined to become the most popular detective in crime fiction since Sherlock Holmes. It was eventually published by The Bodley Head in 1920.

In 1926, after averaging a book a year, Agatha Christie wrote her masterpiece. *The Murder of Roger Ackroyd* was the first of her books to be published by Collins and marked the beginning of an author-publisher relationship which lasted for 50 years and well over 70 books. *The Murder of Roger Ackroyd* was also the first of Agatha Christie's books to be dramatised – under the name *Alibi* – and to have a successful run in London's West End. *The Mousetrap*, her most famous play of all, opened in 1952 and is the longest-running play in history.

Agatha Christie was made a Dame in 1971. She died in 1976, since when a number of books have been published posthumously: the bestselling novel *Sleeping Murder* appeared later that year, followed by her autobiography and the short story collections *Miss Marple's Final Cases*, *Problem at Pollensa Bay* and *While the Light Lasts*. In 1998 *Black Coffee* was the first of her plays to be novelised by another author, Charles Osborne.

The Agatha Christie Collection

The Man In The Brown Suit
The Secret of Chimneys
The Seven Dials Mystery
The Mysterious Mr Quin
The Sittaford Mystery
The Hound of Death
The Listerdale Mystery
Why Didn't They Ask Evans?
Parker Pyne Investigates
Murder Is Easy
And Then There Were None
Death Comes as the End
Sparkling Cyanide
Crooked House
They Came to Baghdad
Destination Unknown
Spider's Web *
The Unexpected Guest *
Ordeal by Innocence
The Pale Horse
Endless Night
Passenger To Frankfurt

Poirot
The Mysterious Affair at Styles
Murder on the Links
Poirot Investigates
The Murder of Roger Ackroyd
The Big Four
The Mystery of the Blue Train
Black Coffee *
Peril at End House
Lord Edgware Dies
Murder on the Orient Express
Three Act Tragedy
Death in the Clouds
The ABC Murders
Murder in Mesopotamia
Cards on the Table
Murder in the Mews
Dumb Witness
Death on the Nile
Appointment With Death
Hercule Poirot's Christmas
Sad Cypress
One, Two, Buckle My Shoe
Evil Under the Sun
Five Little Pigs
The Hollow
The Labours of Hercules

* novelised by Charles Osborne

Taken at the Flood
Mrs McGinty's Dead
After the Funeral
Hickory Dickory Dock
Dead Man's Folly
Cat Among the Pigeons
The Adventure of the Christmas Pudding
The Clocks
Third Girl
Hallowe'en Party
Elephants Can Remember
Poirot's Early Cases
Curtain: Poirot's Last Case

Marple
The Murder at the Vicarage
The Thirteen Problems
The Body in the Library
The Moving Finger
A Murder is Announced
They Do It With Mirrors
A Pocket Full of Rye
4.50 from Paddington
The Mirror Crack'd from Side to Side
A Caribbean Mystery
At Bertram's Hotel
Nemesis
Sleeping Murder
Miss Marple's Final Cases

Tommy & Tuppence
The Secret Adversary
Partners in Crime
N or M?
By the Pricking of My Thumbs
Postern of Fate

Published as Mary Westmacott
Giant's Bread
Unfinished Portrait
Absent in the Spring
The Rose and the Yew Tree
A Daughter's a Daughter
The Burden

Memoirs
An Autobiography
Come, Tell Me How You Live

Play Collections
The Mousetrap and Selected Plays
Witness for the Prosecution and Selected Plays

down. 'All cannot be as Hercule Poirot! I know it well.'

'You really have the best opinion of yourself of anyone I ever knew!' I cried, divided between amusement and annoyance.

'What will you? When one is unique, one knows it! And others share that opinion – even, if I mistake it not, Miss Mary Marvell.'

'What?'

'Without doubt. She is coming here.'

'How do you make that out?'

'Very simply. This street, it is not aristocratic, *mon ami*! In it there is no fashionable doctor, no fashionable dentist – still less is there a fashionable milliner! But there *is* a fashionable detective. *Oui*, my friend, it is true – I am become the mode, the *dernier cri!* One says to another: "*Comment?* You have lost your gold pencil-case? You must go to the little Belgian. He is too marvellous! Everyone goes! *Courez!*" And they arrive! In flocks, *mon ami*! With problems of the most foolish!' A bell rang below. 'What did I tell you? That is Miss Marvell.'

As usual, Poirot was right. After a short interval, the American film star was ushered in, and we rose to our feet.

Mary Marvell was undoubtedly one of the most popular actresses on the screen. She had only lately arrived in England in company with her husband, Gregory B. Rolf, also a film actor. Their marriage had taken place about a year ago in the States and this was their first visit to England. They had been given a great reception. Everyone was prepared to go mad over Mary Marvell, her wonderful clothes, her furs, her jewels, above all one jewel, the great diamond which had been nicknamed, to match its owner, 'The Western Star'. Much, true and untrue, had been written about this famous stone which was reported to be insured for the enormous sum of fifty thousand pounds.

All these details passed rapidly through my mind as I joined with Poirot in greeting our fair client.

Miss Marvell was small and slender, very fair and girlish looking, with the wide innocent blue eyes of a child.

Poirot drew forward a chair for her, and she commenced talking at once.

'You will probably think me very foolish, Monsieur Poirot, but Lord Cronshaw was telling me last night how wonderfully you cleared up the mystery of his nephew's death, and I felt that I just must have your advice. I dare say it's only a silly hoax – Gregory says so – but it's just worrying me to death.'

She paused for breath. Poirot beamed encouragement.

'Proceed, madame. You comprehend, I am still in the dark.'

'It's these letters.' Miss Marvell unclasped her handbag, and drew out three envelopes which she handed to Poirot.

The latter scrutinized them closely.

'Cheap paper – the name and address carefully printed. Let us see the inside.' He drew out the enclosure.

I had joined him, and was leaning over his shoulder. The writing consisted of a single sentence, carefully printed like the envelope. It ran as follows:

> *'The great diamond which is the left eye of the god must return whence it came.'*

The second letter was couched in precisely the same terms, but the third was more explicit:

> *'You have been warned. You have not obeyed. Now the diamond will be taken from you. At the full of the moon, the two diamonds which are the left and right eye of the god shall return. So it is written.'*

'The first letter I treated as a joke,' explained Miss Marvell. 'When I got the second, I began to wonder.

The third one came yesterday, and it seemed to me that, after all, the matter might be more serious than I had imagined.'

'I see they did not come by post, these letters.'

'No; they were left by hand – by a *Chinaman*. That is what frightens me.'

'Why?'

'Because it was from a Chink in San Francisco that Gregory bought the stone three years ago.'

'I see, madame, that you believe the diamond referred to to be –'

'"The Western Star,"' finished Miss Marvell. 'That's so. At the time, Gregory remembers that there was some story attached to the stone, but the Chink wasn't handing out any information. Gregory says he seemed just scared to death, and in a mortal hurry to get rid of the thing. He only asked about a tenth of its value. It was Greg's wedding present to me.'

Poirot nodded thoughtfully.

'The story seems of an almost unbelievable romanticism. And yet – who knows? I pray of you, Hastings, hand me my little almanac.'

I complied.

'*Voyons!*' said Poirot, turning the leaves. 'When is the date of the full moon? Ah, Friday next. That is in three days' time. *Eh bien*, madame, you seek my advice – I give it to you. This *belle histoire* may be a hoax –

but it may not! Therefore I counsel you to place the diamond in my keeping until after Friday next. Then we can take what steps we please.'

A slight cloud passed over the actress's face, and she replied constrainedly:

'I'm afraid that's impossible.'

'You have it with you – *hein?*' Poirot was watching her narrowly.

The girl hesitated a moment, then slipped her hand into the bosom of her gown, drawing out a long thin chain. She leaned forward, unclosing her hand. In the palm, a stone of white fire, exquisitely set in platinum, lay and winked at us solemnly.

Poirot drew in his breath with a long hiss.

'*Épatant!*' he murmured. 'You permit, madame?' He took the jewel in his own hand and scrutinized it keenly, then restored it to her with a little bow. 'A magnificent stone – without a flaw. Ah, *cent tonnerres!* and you carry it about with you, *comme ça!*'

'No, no, I'm very careful really, Monsieur Poirot. As a rule it's locked up in my jewel-case, and left in the hotel safe deposit. We're staying at the *Magnificent*, you know. I just brought it along today for you to see.'

'And you will leave it with me, *n'est-ce pas?* You will be advised by Papa Poirot?'

'Well, you see, it's this way, Monsieur Poirot. On

13

Friday we're going down to Yardly Chase to spend a few days with Lord and Lady Yardly.'

Her words awoke a vague echo of remembrance in my mind. Some gossip – what was it now? A few years ago Lord and Lady Yardly had paid a visit to the States, rumour had it that his lordship had rather gone the pace out there with the assistance of some lady friends – but surely there was something more, more gossip which coupled Lady Yardly's name with that of a 'movie' star in California – why! it came to me in a flash – of course it was none other than Gregory B. Rolf.

'I'll let you into a little secret, Monsieur Poirot,' Miss Marvell was continuing. 'We've got a deal on with Lord Yardly. There's some chance of our arranging to film a play down there in his ancestral pile.'

'At Yardly Chase?' I cried, interested. 'Why, it's one of the showplaces of England.'

Miss Marvell nodded.

'I guess it's the real old feudal stuff all right. But he wants a pretty stiff price, and of course I don't know yet whether the deal will go through, but Greg and I always like to combine business with pleasure.'

'But – I demand pardon if I am dense, madame – surely it is possible to visit Yardly Chase without taking the diamond with you?'

A shrewd, hard look came into Miss Marvell's eyes

which belied their childlike appearance. She looked suddenly a good deal older.

'I want to wear it down there.'

'Surely,' I said suddenly, 'there are some very famous jewels in the Yardly collection, a large diamond amongst them?'

'That's so,' said Miss Marvell briefly.

I heard Poirot murmur beneath his breath: 'Ah, *c'est comme ça!*' Then he said aloud, with his usual uncanny luck in hitting the bull's-eye (he dignifies it by the name of psychology): 'Then you are without doubt already acquainted with Lady Yardly, or perhaps your husband is?'

'Gregory knew her when she was out West three years ago,' said Miss Marvell. She hesitated a moment, and then added abruptly: 'Do either of you ever see *Society Gossip?*'

We both pleaded guilty rather shamefacedly.

'I ask because in this week's number there is an article on famous jewels, and it's really very curious –' She broke off.

I rose, went to the table at the other side of the room and returned with the paper in question in my hand. She took it from me, found the article, and began to read aloud:

'. . . Amongst other famous stones may be included The

15

Star of the East, a diamond in the possession of the Yardly family. An ancestor of the present Lord Yardly brought it back with him from China, and a romantic story is said to attach to it. According to this, the stone was once the right eye of a temple god. Another diamond, exactly similar in form and size, formed the left eye, and the story goes that this jewel, too, would in course of time be stolen. "One eye shall go West, the other East, till they shall meet once more. Then, in triumph shall they return to the god." It is a curious coincidence that there is at the present time a stone corresponding closely in description with this one, and known as 'The Star of the West', or 'The Western Star'. It is the property of the celebrated film star, Miss Mary Marvell. A comparison of the two stones would be interesting.'

She stopped.

'*Épatant!*' murmured Poirot. 'Without doubt a romance of the first water.' He turned to Mary Marvell. 'And you are not afraid, madame? You have no superstitious terrors? You do not fear to introduce these two Siamese twins to each other lest a Chinaman should appear and, hey presto! whisk them both back to China?'

His tone was mocking, but I fancied that an undercurrent of seriousness lay beneath it.

'I don't believe that Lady Yardly's diamond is anything

like as good as mine,' said Miss Marvell. 'Anyway, I'm going to see.'

What more Poirot would have said I do not know, for at that moment the door flew open, and a splendid-looking man strode into the room. From his crisply curling black head, to the tips of his patent-leather boots, he was a hero fit for romance.

'I said I'd call round for you, Mary,' said Gregory Rolf, 'and here I am. Well, what does Monsieur Poirot say to our little problem? Just one big hoax, same as I do?'

Poirot smiled up at the big actor. They made a ridiculous contrast.

'Hoax or no hoax, Mr Rolf,' he said dryly, 'I have advised Madame your wife not to take the jewel with her to Yardly Chase on Friday.'

'I'm with you there, sir. I've already said so to Mary. But there! She's a woman through and through, and I guess she can't bear to think of another woman outshining her in the jewel line.'

'What nonsense, Gregory!' said Mary Marvell sharply. But she flushed angrily.

Poirot shrugged his shoulders.

'Madame, I have advised. I can do no more. *C'est fini.*'

He bowed them both to the door.

'Ah! *la la*,' he observed, returning. '*Histoire des femmes!* The good husband, he hit the nail – *tout de*

Agatha Christie

même, but he was not tactful! Assuredly not.'

I imparted to him my vague remembrances, and he nodded vigorously.

'So I thought. All the same, there is something curious underneath all this. With your permission, *mon ami*, I will take the air. Await my return, I beg of you, I shall not be long.'

I was half asleep in my chair when the landlady tapped on the door, and put her head in.

'It's another lady to see Mr Poirot, sir. I've told her he was out, but she says as how she'll wait, seeing as she's come up from the country.'

'Oh, show her in here, Mrs Murchinson. Perhaps I can do something for her.'

In another moment the lady had been ushered in. My heart gave a leap as I recognized her. Lady Yardly's portrait had figured too often in the Society papers to allow her to remain unknown.

'Do sit down, Lady Yardly,' I said, drawing forward a chair. 'My friend, Poirot, is out, but I know for a fact that he'll be back very shortly.'

She thanked me and sat down. A very different type, this, from Miss Mary Marvell. Tall, dark, with flashing eyes, and a pale proud face – yet something wistful in the curves of the mouth.

I felt a desire to rise to the occasion. Why not? In Poirot's presence I have frequently felt a difficulty – I do not appear at my best. And yet there is no doubt that I, too, possess the deductive sense in a marked degree. I leant forward on a sudden impulse.

'Lady Yardly,' I said, 'I know why you have come here. You have received blackmailing letters about the diamond.'

There was no doubt as to my bolt having shot home. She stared at me open-mouthed, all colour banished from her cheeks.

'You know?' she gasped. 'How?'

I smiled.

'By a perfectly logical process. If Miss Marvell has had warning letters –'

'Miss Marvell? She has been here?'

'She has just left. As I was saying, if she, as the holder of one of the twin diamonds, has received a mysterious series of warnings, you, as the holder of the other stone, must necessarily have done the same. You see how simple it is? I am right, then, you have received these strange communications also?'

For a moment she hesitated, as though in doubt whether to trust me or not, then she bowed her head in assent with a little smile.

'That is so,' she acknowledged.

'Were yours, too, left by hand – by a Chinaman?'

'No, they came by post; but tell me, has Miss Marvell undergone the same experience, then?'

19

Agatha Christie

I recounted to her the events of the morning. She listened attentively.

'It all fits in. My letters are the duplicate of hers. It is true that they came by post, but there is a curious perfume impregnating them – something in the nature of joss-stick – that at once suggested the East to me. What does it all mean?'

I shook my head.

'That is what we must find out. You have the letters with you? We might learn something from the postmarks.'

'Unfortunately I destroyed them. You understand, at the time I regarded it as some foolish joke. Can it be true that some Chinese gang are really trying to recover the diamonds? It seems too incredible.'

We went over the facts again and again, but could get no further towards the elucidation of the mystery. At last Lady Yardly rose.

'I really don't think I need wait for Monsieur Poirot. You can tell him all this, can't you? Thank you so much Mr –'

She hesitated, her hand outstretched.

'Captain Hastings.'

'Of course! How stupid of me. You're a friend of the Cavendishes, aren't you? It was Mary Cavendish who sent me to Monsieur Poirot.'

When my friend returned, I enjoyed telling him the tale of what had occurred during his absence. He cross-questioned me rather sharply over the details of our conversation and I could read between the lines that he was not best pleased to have been absent. I also fancied that the dear old fellow was just the least inclined to be jealous. It had become rather a pose with him to consistently belittle my abilities, and I think he was chagrined at finding no loophole for criticism. I was secretly rather pleased with myself, though I tried to conceal the fact for fear of irritating him. In spite of his idiosyncrasies, I was deeply attached to my quaint little friend.

'*Bien!*' he said at length, with a curious look on his face. 'The plot develops. Pass me, I pray you, that *Peerage* on the top shelf there.' He turned the leaves. 'Ah, here we are! "Yardly . . . 10th viscount, served South African War" . . . *tout ça n'a pas d'importance* . . . "mar. 1907 Hon. Maude Stopperton, fourth daughter of 3rd Baron Cotteril" . . . um, um, um . . . "has iss. two daughters, born 1908, 1910 . . . Clubs, residences" . . . *Voilà*, that does not tell us much. But tomorrow morning we see this *milord*!'

'What?'

'Yes. I telephoned to him.'

'I thought you had washed your hands of the case?'

'I am not acting for Miss Marvell since she refuses

21

to be guided by my advice. What I do now is for my own satisfaction – the satisfaction of Hercule Poirot! Decidedly, I must have a finger in this pie.'

'And you calmly wire Lord Yardly to dash up to town just to suit your convenience. He won't be pleased.'

'*Au contraire*, if I preserve for him his family diamond, he ought to be very grateful.'

'Then you really think there is any chance of it being stolen?' I asked eagerly.

'Almost a certainty,' replied Poirot placidly. 'Everything points that way.'

'But how –'

Poirot stopped my eager questions with an airy gesture of the hand.

'Not now, I pray you. Let us not confuse the mind. And observe that *Peerage* – how you have replaced him! See you not that the tallest books go in the top shelf, the next tallest in the row beneath, and so on. Thus we have order, *method*, which, as I have often told you, Hastings –'

'Exactly,' I said hastily, and put the offending volume in its proper place.

II

Lord Yardly turned out to be a cheery, loud-voiced sportsman with a rather red face, but with a good-humoured bonhomie about him that was distinctly attractive and made up for any lack of mentality.

'Extraordinary business this, Monsieur Poirot. Can't make head or tail of it. Seems my wife's been getting odd kind of letters, and that Miss Marvell's had 'em too. What does it all mean?'

Poirot handed him the copy of *Society Gossip*.

'First, *milord*, I would ask you if these facts are substantially correct?'

The peer took it. His face darkened with anger as he read.

'Damned nonsense!' he spluttered. 'There's never been any romantic story attaching to the diamond. It came from India originally, I believe. I never heard of all this Chinese god stuff.'

'Still, the stone is known as "The Star of the East".'

'Well, what if it is?' he demanded wrathfully.

Poirot smiled a little, but made no direct reply.

'What I would ask you to do, *milord*, is to place yourself in my hands. If you do so unreservedly, I have great hopes of averting the catastrophe.'

23

'Then you think there's actually something in these wildcat tales?'

'Will you do as I ask you?'

'Of course I will, but –'

'*Bien!* Then permit that I ask you a few questions. This affair of Yardly Chase, is it, as you say, all fixed up between you and Mr Rolf?'

'Oh, he told you about it, did he? No, there's nothing settled.' He hesitated, the brick-red colour of his face deepening. 'Might as well get the thing straight. I've made rather an ass of myself in many ways, Monsieur Poirot – and I'm head over ears in debt – but I want to pull up. I'm fond of the kids, and I want to straighten things up, and be able to live on at the old place. Gregory Rolf is offering me big money – enough to set me on my feet again. I don't want to do it – I hate the thought of all that crowd play-acting round the Chase – but I may have to, unless –' He broke off.

Poirot eyed him keenly. 'You have, then, another string to your bow? Permit that I make a guess? It is to sell The Star of the East?'

Lord Yardly nodded. 'That's it. It's been in the family for some generations, but it's not essential. Still, it's not the easiest thing in the world to find a purchaser. Hoffberg, the Hatton Garden man, is on the lookout for a likely customer, but he'll have to find one soon, or it's a washout.'

'One more question, *permettez* – Lady Yardly, which plan does she approve?'

'Oh, she's bitterly opposed to my selling the jewel. You know what women are. She's all for this film stunt.'

'I comprehend,' said Poirot. He remained a moment or so in thought, then rose briskly to his feet. 'You return to Yardly Chase at once? *Bien!* Say no word to anyone – to *anyone*, mind – but expect us there this evening. We will arrive shortly after five.

'All right, but I don't see –'

'*Ça n'a pas d'importance*,' said Poirot kindly. 'You will that I preserve for you your diamond, *n'est-ce pas?*'

'Yes, but –'

'Then do as I say.'

A sadly bewildered nobleman left the room.

III

It was half-past five when we arrived at Yardly Chase, and followed the dignified butler to the old panelled hall with its fire of blazing logs. A pretty picture met our eyes: Lady Yardly and her two children, the mother's proud dark head bent down over the two fair ones. Lord Yardly stood near, smiling down on them.

25

'Monsieur Poirot and Captain Hastings,' announced the butler.

Lady Yardly looked up with a start, for her husband came forward uncertainly, his eyes seeking instruction from Poirot. The little man was equal to the occasion.

'All my excuses! It is that I investigate still this affair of Miss Marvell's. She comes to you on Friday, does she not? I make a little tour first to make sure that all is secure. Also I wanted to ask Lady Yardly if she recollected at all the postmarks on the letters she received?'

Lady Yardly shook her head regretfully. 'I'm afraid I don't. It's stupid of me. But, you see, I never dreamt of taking them seriously.'

'You'll stay the night?' said Lord Yardly.

'Oh, *milord*, I fear to incommode you. We have left our bags at the inn.'

'That's all right.' Lord Yardly had his cue. 'We'll send down for them. No, no – no trouble, I assure you.'

Poirot permitted himself to be persuaded, and sitting down by Lady Yardly, began to make friends with the children. In a short time they were all romping together, and had dragged me into the game.

'*Vous êtes bonne mère*,' said Poirot, with a gallant little bow, as the children were removed reluctantly by a stern nurse.

Lady Yardly smoothed her ruffled hair.

'I adore them,' she said with a little catch in her voice.

'And they you – with reason!' Poirot bowed again.

A dressing-gong sounded, and we rose to go up to our rooms. At that moment the butler emerged with a telegram on a salver which he handed to Lord Yardly. The latter tore it open with a brief word of apology. As he read it he stiffened visibly.

With an ejaculation he handed it to his wife. Then he glanced at my friend.

'Just a minute, Monsieur Poirot, I feel you ought to know about this. It's from Hoffberg. He thinks he's found a customer for the diamond – an American, sailing for the States tomorrow. They're sending down a chap tonight to vet the stone. By Jove, though, if this goes through –' Words failed him.

Lady Yardly had turned away. She still held the telegram in her hand.

'I wish you wouldn't sell it, George,' she said, in a low voice. 'It's been in the family so long.' She waited, as though for a reply, but when none came her face hardened. She shrugged her shoulders. 'I must go and dress. I suppose I had better display "the goods".' She turned to Poirot with a slight grimace. 'It's one of the most hideous necklaces that was ever designed! George has always promised to have the stones reset for me, but it's never been done.' She left the room.

Half an hour later, we three were assembled in the great drawing-room awaiting the lady. It was already a few minutes past the dinner hour.

Suddenly there was a low rustle, and Lady Yardly appeared framed in the doorway, a radiant figure in a long white shimmering dress. Round the column of her neck was a rivulet of fire. She stood there with one hand just touching the necklace.

'Behold the sacrifice,' she said gaily. Her ill-humour seemed to have vanished. 'Wait while I turn the big light on and you shall feast your eyes on the ugliest necklace in England.'

The switches were just outside the door. As she stretched out her hand to them, the incredible thing happened. Suddenly, without any warning, every light was extinguished, the door banged, and from the other side of it came a long-drawn piercing woman's scream.

'My God!' cried Lord Yardly. 'That was Maude's voice! What has happened?'

We rushed blindly for the door, cannoning into each other in the darkness. It was some minutes before we could find it. What a sight met our eyes! Lady Yardly lay senseless on the marble floor, a crimson mark on her white throat where the necklace had been wrenched from her neck.

As we bent over her, uncertain for the moment whether she was dead or alive, her eyelids opened.

'The Chinaman,' she whispered painfully. 'The Chinaman – the side door.'

Lord Yardly sprang up with an oath. I accompanied him, my heart beating wildly. The Chinaman again! The side door in question was a small one in the angle of the wall, not more than a dozen yards from the scene of the tragedy. As we reached it, I gave a cry. There, just short of the threshold, lay the glittering necklace, evidently dropped by the thief in the panic of his flight. I swooped joyously down on it. Then I uttered another cry which Lord Yardly echoed. For in the middle of the necklace was a great gap. The Star of the East was missing!

'That settles it,' I breathed. 'These were no ordinary thieves. This one stone was all they wanted.'

'But how did the fellow get in?'

'Through this door.'

'But it's always locked.'

I shook my head. 'It's not locked now. See.' I pulled it open as I spoke.

As I did so something fluttered to the ground. I picked it up. It was a piece of silk, and the embroidery was unmistakable. It had been torn from a Chinaman's robe.

'In his haste it caught in the door,' I explained. 'Come, hurry. He cannot have gone far as yet.'

But in vain we hunted and searched. In the pitch

29

darkness of the night, the thief had found it easy to make his getaway. We returned reluctantly, and Lord Yardly sent off one of the footmen post-haste to fetch the police.

Lady Yardly, aptly ministered to by Poirot, who is as good as a woman in these matters, was sufficiently recovered to be able to tell her story.

'I was just going to turn on the other light,' she said, 'when a man sprang on me from behind. He tore my necklace from my neck with such force that I fell headlong to the floor. As I fell I saw him disappearing through the side door. Then I realized by the pigtail and the embroidered robe that he was a Chinaman.' She stopped with a shudder.

The butler reappeared. He spoke in a low voice to Lord Yardly.

'A gentleman from Mr Hoffberg's, m'lord. He says you expect him.'

'Good heavens!' cried the distracted nobleman. 'I must see him, I suppose. No, not here, Mullings, in the library.'

I drew Poirot aside.

'Look here, my dear fellow, hadn't we better get back to London?'

'You think so, Hastings? Why?'

'Well' – I coughed delicately – 'things haven't gone very well, have they? I mean, you tell Lord Yardly

to place himself in your hands and all will be well
– and then the diamond vanishes from under your
very nose!'

'True,' said Poirot, rather crestfallen. 'It was not one
of my most striking triumphs.'

This way of describing events almost caused me to
smile, but I stuck to my guns.

'So, having – pardon the expression – rather made
a mess of things, don't you think it would be more
graceful to leave immediately?'

'And the dinner, the without doubt excellent dinner,
that the *chef* of Lord Yardly has prepared?'

'Oh, what's dinner!' I said impatiently.

Poirot held up his hands in horror.

'*Mon Dieu!* It is that in this country you treat the
affairs gastronomic with a criminal indifference.'

'There's another reason why we should get back to
London as soon as possible,' I continued.

'What is that, my friend?'

'The other diamond,' I said, lowering my voice.
'Miss Marvell's.'

'*Eh bien*, what of it?'

'Don't you see?' His unusual obtuseness annoyed
me. What had happened to his usually keen wits?
'They've got one, now they'll go for the other.'

'*Tiens!*' cried Poirot, stepping back a pace and
regarding me with admiration. 'But your brain marches

31

to a marvel, my friend! Figure to yourself that for the moment I had not thought of that! But there is plenty of time. The full of the moon, it is not until Friday.'

I shook my head dubiously. The full of the moon theory left me entirely cold. I had my way with Poirot, however, and we departed immediately, leaving behind us a note of explanation and apology for Lord Yardly.

My idea was to go at once to the *Magnificent*, and relate to Miss Marvell what had occurred, but Poirot vetoed the plan, and insisted that the morning would be time enough. I gave in rather grudgingly.

In the morning Poirot seemed strangely disinclined to stir out. I began to suspect that, having made a mistake to start with, he was singularly loath to proceed with the case. In answer to my persuasions, he pointed out, with admirable common sense, that as the details of the affair at Yardly Chase were already in the morning papers the Rolfs would know quite as much as we could tell them. I gave way unwillingly.

Events proved my forebodings to be justified. About two o'clock, the telephone rang. Poirot answered it. He listened for some moments, then with a brief '*Bien, j'y serai*' he rang off, and turned to me.

'What do you think, *mon ami*?' He looked half ashamed, half excited. 'The diamond of Miss Marvell, it has been stolen.'

'What?' I cried, springing up. 'And what about the

"full of the moon" now?' Poirot hung his head. 'When did this happen?'

'This morning, I understand.'

I shook my head sadly. 'If only you had listened to me. You see I was right.'

'It appears so, *mon ami*,' said Poirot cautiously. 'Appearances are deceptive, they say, but it certainly appears so.'

As we hurried in a taxi to the *Magnificent*, I puzzled out the true inwardness of the scheme.

'That "full of the moon" idea was clever. The whole point of it was to get us to concentrate on the Friday, and so be off our guard beforehand. It is a pity you did not realize that.'

'*Ma foi!*' said Poirot airily, his nonchalance quite restored after its brief eclipse. 'One cannot think of everything!'

I felt sorry for him. He did so hate failure of any kind.

'Cheer up,' I said consolingly. 'Better luck next time.'

At the *Magnificent*, we were ushered at once into the manager's office. Gregory Rolf was there with two men from Scotland Yard. A pale-faced clerk sat opposite them.

Rolf nodded to us as we entered.

'We're getting to the bottom of it,' he said. 'But

it's almost unbelievable. How the guy had the nerve I can't think.'

A very few minutes sufficed to give us the facts. Mr Rolf had gone out of the hotel at 11.15. At 11.30, a gentleman, so like him in appearance as to pass muster, entered the hotel and demanded the jewel-case from the safe deposit. He duly signed the receipt, remarking carelessly as he did so: 'Looks a bit different from my ordinary one, but I hurt my hand getting out of the taxi.' The clerk merely smiled and remarked that he saw very little difference. Rolf laughed and said: 'Well, don't run me in as a crook this time, anyway. I've been getting threatening letters from a Chinaman, and the worst of it is I look rather like a Chink myself – it's something about the eyes.'

'I looked at him,' said the clerk who was telling us this, 'and I saw at once what he meant. The eyes slanted up at the corners like an Oriental's. I'd never noticed it before.'

'Darn it all, man,' roared Gregory Rolf, leaning forward, 'do you notice it now?'

The man looked up at him and started.

'No, sir,' he said. 'I can't say I do.' And indeed there was nothing even remotely Oriental about the frank brown eyes that looked into ours.

The Scotland Yard man grunted. 'Bold customer. Thought the eyes might be noticed, and took the bull by the horns to disarm suspicion. He must have watched you out of the hotel, sir, and nipped in as soon as you were well away.'

'What about the jewel-case?' I asked.

'It was found in the corridor of the hotel. Only one thing had been taken – "The Western Star".'

We stared at each other – the whole thing was so bizarre, so unreal.

Poirot hopped briskly to his feet. 'I have not been of much use, I fear,' he said regretfully. 'Is it permitted to see Madame?'

'I guess she's prostrated with the shock,' exclaimed Rolf.

'Then perhaps I might have a few words alone with you, monsieur?'

'Certainly.'

In about five minutes Poirot reappeared.

'Now, my friend,' he said gaily. 'To a post office. I have to send a telegram.'

'Who to?'

'Lord Yardly.' He discounted further inquiries by slipping his arm through mine. 'Come, come, *mon ami*. I know all that you feel about this terrible business. I have not distinguished myself! You, in my place, might have distinguished yourself. *Bien!* All is admitted. Let us forget it and have lunch.'

It was about four o'clock when we entered Poirot's

rooms. A figure rose from a chair by the window. It was Lord Yardly. He looked haggard and distraught.

'I got your wire and came up at once. Look here, I've been round to Hoffberg, and they know nothing about that man of theirs last night, or the wire either. Do you think that –'

Poirot held up his hand.

'My excuses! I sent that wire, and hired the gentleman in question.'

'*You* – but why? What?' The nobleman spluttered impotently.

'My little idea was to bring things to a head,' explained Poirot placidly.

'Bring things to a head! Oh, my God!' cried Lord Yardly.

'And the ruse succeeded,' said Poirot cheerfully. 'Therefore, *milord*, I have much pleasure in returning you – this!' With a dramatic gesture he produced a glittering object. It was a great diamond.

'The Star of the East,' gasped Lord Yardly. 'But I don't understand –'

'No?' said Poirot. 'It makes no matter. Believe me, it was necessary for the diamond to be stolen. I promised you that it would be preserved to you, and I have kept my word. You must permit me to keep my little secret. Convey, I beg of you, the assurance of my deepest respect to Lady Yardly, and tell her how pleased I am to be able to restore her jewel to her. What *beau temps*, is it not? Good day, *milord*.'

And smiling and talking, the amazing little man conducted the bewildered nobleman to the door. He returned gently rubbing his hands.

'Poirot,' I said. 'Am I quite demented?'

'No, *mon ami*, but you are, as always, in a mental fog.'

'How did you get the diamond?'

'From Mr Rolf.'

'Rolf?'

'*Mais oui!* The warning letters, the Chinaman, the article in *Society Gossip*, all sprang from the ingenious brain of Mr Rolf! The two diamonds, supposed to be so miraculously alike – bah! they did not exist. There was only *one* diamond, my friend! Originally in the Yardly collection, for three years it has been in the possession of Mr Rolf. He stole it this morning with the assistance of a touch of grease paint at the corner of each eye! Ah, I must see him on the film, he is indeed an artist, *celui-là*!'

'But why should he steal his own diamond?' I asked, puzzled.

'For many reasons. To begin with, Lady Yardly was getting restive.'

'Lady Yardly?'

'You comprehend she was left much alone in

Agatha Christie

California. Her husband was amusing himself elsewhere. Mr Rolf was handsome, he had an air about him of romance. But *au fond*, he is very businesslike, *ce monsieur*! He made love to Lady Yardly, and then he blackmailed her. I taxed the lady with the truth the other night, and she admitted it. She swore that she had only been indiscreet, and I believe her. But, undoubtedly, Rolf had letters of hers that could be twisted to bear a different interpretation. Terrified by the threat of a divorce, and the prospect of being separated from her children, she agreed to all he wished. She had no money of her own, and she was forced to permit him to substitute a paste replica for the real stone. The coincidence of the date of the appearance of "The Western Star" struck me at once. All goes well. Lord Yardly prepares to range himself – to settle down. And then comes the menace of the possible sale of the diamond. The substitution will be discovered. Without doubt she writes off frantically to Gregory Rolf who has just arrived in England. He soothes her by promising to arrange all – and prepares for a double robbery. In this way he will quiet the lady, who might conceivably tell all to her husband, an affair which would not suit our blackmailer at all, he will have £50,000 insurance money (aha, you had forgotten that!), and he will still have the diamond! At this point I put my fingers in the pie. The arrival of a diamond expert is announced. Lady Yardly, as I felt sure she would, immediately arranges a robbery – and does it very well too! But Hercule Poirot, he sees nothing but facts. What happens in actuality? The lady switches off the light, bangs the door, throws the necklace down the passage, and screams. She has already wrenched out the diamond with pliers upstairs –'

'But we saw the necklace round her neck!' I objected.

'I demand pardon, my friend. Her hand concealed the part of it where the gap would have shown. To place a piece of silk in the door beforehand is child's play! Of course, as soon as Rolf read of the robbery, he arranged his own little comedy. And very well he played it!'

'What did you say to him?' I asked with lively curiosity.

'I said to him that Lady Yardly had told her husband all, that I was empowered to recover the jewel, and that if it were not immediately handed over proceedings would be taken. Also a few more little lies which occurred to me. He was as wax in my hands!'

I pondered the matter.

'It seems a little unfair on Mary Marvell. She has lost her diamond through no fault of her own.'

'Bah!' said Poirot brutally. 'She has a magnificent advertisement. That is all she cares for, that one! Now the other, she is different. *Bonne mère, très femme!*'

'Yes,' I said doubtfully, hardly sharing Poirot's views on femininity. 'I suppose it was Rolf who sent her the duplicate letters.'

'*Pas du tout*,' said Poirot briskly. 'She came by the advice of Mary Cavendish to seek my aid in her dilemma. Then she heard that Mary Marvell, whom she knew to be her enemy, had been here, and she changed her mind jumping at a pretext that *you*, my friend, offered her. A very few questions sufficed to show me that *you* told her of the letters, not she you! She jumped at the chance your words offered.'

'I don't believe it,' I cried, stung.

'*Si, si, mon ami*, it is a pity that you study not the psychology. She told you that the letters were destroyed? Oh, *la la*, *never* does a woman destroy a letter if she can avoid it! Not even if it would be more prudent to do so!'

'It's all very well,' I said, my anger rising, 'but you've made a perfect fool of me! From beginning to end! No, it's all very well to try and explain it away afterwards. There really is a limit!'

'But you were so enjoying yourself, my friend, I had not the heart to shatter your illusions.'

'It's no good. You've gone a bit too far this time.'

'*Mon Dieu!* but how you enrage yourself for nothing, *mon ami*!'

'I'm fed up!' I went out, banging the door. Poirot

had made an absolute laughing-stock of me. I decided that he needed a sharp lesson. I would let some time elapse before I forgave him. He had encouraged me to make a perfect fool of myself.

Part 2

The Tragedy at Marsdon Manor

I had been called away from town for a few days, and on my return found Poirot in the act of strapping up his small valise.

'*A la bonne heure*, Hastings, I feared you would not have returned in time to accompany me.'

'You are called away on a case, then?'

'Yes, though I am bound to admit that, on the face of it, the affair does not seem promising. The Northern Union Insurance Company have asked me to investigate the death of a Mr Maltravers who a few weeks ago insured his life with them for the large sum of fifty thousand pounds.'

'Yes?' I said, much interested.

'There was, of course, the usual suicide clause in the policy. In the event of his committing suicide within a year the premiums would be forfeited. Mr Maltravers was duly examined by the Company's own

Agatha Christie

doctor, and although he was a man slightly past the prime of life was passed as being in quite sound health. However, on Wednesday last – the day before yesterday – the body of Mr Maltravers was found in the grounds of his house in Essex, Marsdon Manor, and the cause of his death is described as some kind of internal haemorrhage. That in itself would be nothing remarkable, but sinister rumours as to Mr Maltravers' financial position have been in the air of late, and the Northern Union have ascertained beyond any possible doubt that the deceased gentleman stood upon the verge of bankruptcy. Now that alters matters considerably. Maltravers had a beautiful young wife, and it is suggested that he got together all the ready money he could for the purpose of paying the premiums on a life insurance for his wife's benefit, and then committed suicide. Such a thing is not uncommon. In any case, my friend Alfred Wright, who is a director of the Northern Union, has asked me to investigate the facts of the case, but, as I told him, I am not very hopeful of success. If the cause of the death had been heart failure, I should have been more sanguine. Heart failure may always be translated as the inability of the local GP to discover what his patient really did die of, but a haemorrhage seems fairly definite. Still, we can but make some necessary inquiries. Five minutes to pack your bag, Hastings, and we will take a taxi to Liverpool Street.'

About an hour later, we alighted from a Great Eastern train at the little station of Marsdon Leigh. Inquiries at the station yielded the information that Marsdon Manor was about a mile distant. Poirot decided to walk, and we betook ourselves along the main street.

'What is our plan of campaign?' I asked.

'First I will call upon the doctor. I have ascertained that there is only one doctor in Marsdon Leigh, Dr Ralph Bernard. Ah, here we are at his house.'

The house in question was a kind of superior cottage, standing back a little from the road. A brass plate on the gate bore the doctor's name. We passed up the path and rang the bell.

We proved to be fortunate in our call. It was the doctor's consulting hour, and for the moment there were no patients waiting for him. Dr Bernard was an elderly man, high-shouldered and stooping, with a pleasant vagueness of manner.

Poirot introduced himself and explained the purpose of our visit, adding that Insurance Companies were bound to investigate fully in a case of this kind.

'Of course, of course,' said Dr Bernard vaguely. 'I suppose, as he was such a rich man, his life was insured for a big sum?'

'You consider him a rich man, doctor?'

The doctor looked rather surprised.

'Was he not? He kept two cars, you know, and Marsden Manor is a pretty big place to keep up, although I believe he bought it very cheap.'

'I understand that he had had considerable losses of late,' said Poirot, watching the doctor narrowly.

The latter, however, merely shook his head sadly.

'Is that so? Indeed. It is fortunate for his wife, then, that there is this life insurance. A very beautiful and charming young creature, but terribly unstrung by this sad catastrophe. A mass of nerves, poor thing. I have tried to spare her all I can, but of course the shock was bound to be considerable.'

'You had been attending Mr Maltravers recently?'

'My dear sir, I never attended him.'

'What?'

'I understand Mr Maltravers was a Christian Scientist – or something of that kind.'

'But you examined the body?'

'Certainly. I was fetched by one of the under-gardeners.'

'And the cause of death was clear?'

'Absolutely. There was blood on the lips, but most of the bleeding must have been internal.'

'Was he still lying where he had been found?'

'Yes, the body had not been touched. He was lying at the edge of a small plantation. He had evidently been out shooting rooks, a small rook rifle lay beside him.

The haemorrhage must have occurred quite suddenly. Gastric ulcer, without a doubt.'

'No question of his having been shot, eh?'

'My dear sir!'

'I demand pardon,' said Poirot humbly. 'But, if my memory is not at fault, in the case of a recent murder, the doctor first gave a verdict of heart failure – altering it when the local constable pointed out that there was a bullet wound through the head!'

'You will not find any bullet wounds on the body of Mr Maltravers,' said Dr Bernard dryly. 'Now gentlemen, if there is nothing further –'

We took the hint.

'Good morning, and many thanks to you, doctor, for so kindly answering our questions. By the way, you saw no need for an autopsy?'

'Certainly not.' The doctor became quite apoplectic. 'The cause of death was clear, and in my profession we see no need to distress unduly the relatives of a dead patient.'

And, turning, the doctor slammed the door sharply in our faces.

'And what do you think of Dr Bernard, Hastings?' inquired Poirot, as we proceeded on our way to the Manor.

'Rather an old ass.'

'Exactly. Your judgements of character are always profound, my friend.'

I glanced at him uneasily, but he seemed perfectly serious. A twinkle, however, came into his eye, and he added slyly:

'That is to say, where there is no question of a beautiful woman!'

I looked at him coldly.

On our arrival at the manor house, the door was opened to us by a middle-aged parlourmaid. Poirot handed her his card, and a letter from the Insurance Company for Mrs Maltravers. She showed us into a small morning room, and retired to tell her mistress. About ten minutes elapsed, and then the door opened, and a slender figure in widow's weeds stood upon the threshold.

'Monsieur Poirot?' she faltered.

'Madame!' Poirot sprang gallantly to his feet and hastened towards her. 'I cannot tell you how I regret to derange you in this way. But what will you? *Les affaires* – they know no mercy.'

Mrs Maltravers permitted him to lead her to a chair. Her eyes were red with weeping, but the temporary disfigurement could not conceal her extraordinary beauty. She was about twenty-seven or -eight, and very fair, with large blue eyes and a pretty pouting mouth.

'It is something about my husband's insurance, is it? But must I be bothered *now* – so soon?'

'Courage, my dear madame. Courage! You see, your

late husband insured his life for rather a large sum, and in such a case the Company always has to satisfy itself as to a few details. They have empowered me to act for them. You can rest assured that I will do all in my power to render the matter not too unpleasant for you. Will you recount to me briefly the sad events of Wednesday?'

'I was changing for tea when my maid came up – one of the gardeners had just run to the house. He had found –'

Her voice trailed away. Poirot pressed her hand sympathetically.

'I comprehend. Enough! You had seen your husband earlier in the afternoon?'

'Not since lunch. I had walked down to the village for some stamps, and I believe he was out pottering round the grounds.'

'Shooting rooks, eh?'

'Yes, he usually took his little rook rifle with him, and I heard one or two shots in the distance.'

'Where is this little rook rifle now?'

'In the hall, I think.'

She led the way out of the room and found and handed the little weapon to Poirot, who examined it cursorily.

'Two shots fired, I see,' he observed, as he handed it back. 'And now, madame, if I might see –'

He paused delicately.

'The servant shall take you,' she murmured, averting her head.

The parlourmaid, summoned, led Poirot upstairs. I remained with the lovely and unfortunate woman. It was hard to know whether to speak or remain silent. I essayed one or two general reflections to which she responded absently, and in a very few minutes Poirot rejoined us.

'I thank you for all your courtesy, madame. I do not think you need be troubled any further with this matter. By the way, do you know anything of your husband's financial position?'

She shook her head.

'Nothing whatever. I am very stupid over business things.'

'I see. Then you can give us no clue as to why he suddenly decided to insure his life? He had not done so previously, I understand.'

'Well, we had only been married a little over a year. But, as to why he insured his life, it was because he had absolutely made up his mind that he would not live long. He had a strong premonition of his own death. I gather that he had had one haemorrhage already, and that he knew that another one would prove fatal. I tried to dispel these gloomy fears of his, but without avail. Alas, he was only too right!'

Tears in her eyes, she bade us a dignified farewell.

Poirot made a characteristic gesture as we walked down the drive together.

'*Eh bien*, that is that! Back to London, my friend, there appears to be no mouse in this mouse-hole. And yet –'

'Yet what?'

'A slight discrepancy, that is all! You noticed it? You did not? Still, life is full of discrepancies, and assuredly the man cannot have taken his life – there is no poison that would fill his mouth with blood. No, no, I must resign myself to the fact that all here is clear and above board – but who is this?'

A tall young man was striding up the drive towards us. He passed us without making any sign, but I noted that he was not ill-looking, with a lean, deeply-bronzed face that spoke of life in a tropic clime. A gardener who was sweeping up leaves had paused for a minute in his task, and Poirot ran quickly up to him.

'Tell me, I pray you, who is that gentleman? Do you know him?'

'I don't remember his name, sir, though I did hear it. He was staying down here last week for a night. Tuesday, it was.'

'Quick, *mon ami*, let us follow him.'

We hastened up the drive after the retreating figure. A glimpse of a black-robed figure on the terrace at the side of the house, and our quarry swerved and we after him, so that we were witnesses of the meeting.

Mrs Maltravers almost staggered where she stood, and her face blanched noticeably.

'You,' she gasped. 'I thought you were on the sea – on your way to East Africa?'

'I got some news from my lawyers that detained me,' explained the young man. 'My old uncle in Scotland died unexpectedly and left me some money. Under the circumstances I thought it better to cancel my passage. Then I saw this bad news in the paper and I came down to see if there was anything I could do. You'll want someone to look after things for you a bit perhaps.'

At that moment they became aware of our presence. Poirot stepped forward, and with many apologies explained that he had left his stick in the hall. Rather reluctantly, it seemed to me, Mrs Maltravers made the necessary introduction.

'Monsieur Poirot, Captain Black.'

A few minutes' chat ensued, in the course of which Poirot elicited the fact that Captain Black was putting up at the Anchor Inn. The missing stick not having been discovered (which was not surprising), Poirot uttered more apologies and we withdrew.

We returned to the village at a great pace, and Poirot made a beeline for the Anchor Inn.

'Here we establish ourselves until our friend the Captain returns,' he explained. 'You noticed that I emphasized the point that we were returning to London by the first train? Possibly you thought I meant it. But no – you observed Mrs Maltravers' face when she caught sight of this young Black? She was clearly taken aback, and he – *eh bien*, he was very devoted, did you not think so? And he was here on Tuesday night – the day before Mr Maltravers died. We must investigate the doings of Captain Black, Hastings.'

In about half an hour we espied our quarry approaching the inn. Poirot went out and accosted him and presently brought him up to the room we had engaged.

'I have been telling Captain Black of the mission which brings us here,' he explained. 'You can understand, *monsieur le capitaine*, that I am anxious to arrive at Mr Maltravers' state of mind immediately before his death, and that at the same time I do not wish to distress Mrs Maltravers unduly by asking her painful questions. Now, you were here just before the occurrence, and can give us equally valuable information.'

'I'll do anything I can to help you, I'm sure,' replied the young soldier; 'but I'm afraid I didn't notice anything out of the ordinary. You see, although Maltravers was an old friend of my people's, I didn't know him very well myself.'

'You came down – when?'

Agatha Christie

'Tuesday afternoon. I went up to town early Wednesday morning, as my boat sailed from Tilbury about twelve o'clock. But some news I got made me alter my plans, as I dare say you heard me explain to Mrs Maltravers.'

'You were returning to East Africa, I understand?'

'Yes. I've been out there ever since the War – a great country.'

'Exactly. Now what was the talk about at dinner on Tuesday night?'

'Oh, I don't know. The usual odd topics. Maltravers asked after my people, and then we discussed the question of German reparations, and then Mr Maltravers asked a lot of questions about East Africa, and I told them one or two yarns, that's about all, I think.'

'Thank you.'

Poirot was silent for a moment, then he said gently: 'With your permission, I should like to try a little experiment. You have told us all that your conscious self knows, I want now to question your subconscious self.'

'Psychoanalysis, what?' said Black, with visible alarm.

'Oh, no,' said Poirot reassuringly. 'You see, it is like this, I give you a word, you answer with another, and so on. Any word, the first you think of. Shall we begin?'

'All right,' said Black slowly, but he looked uneasy.

'Note down the words, please, Hastings,' said Poirot. Then he took from his pocket his big turnip-faced watch and laid it on the table beside him. 'We will commence. Day.'

There was a moment's pause, and then Black replied: '*Night.*'

As Poirot proceeded, his answers came quicker.

'Name,' said Poirot.

'*Place.*'

'Bernard.'

'*Shaw.*'

'Tuesday.'

'*Dinner.*'

'Journey.'

'*Ship.*'

'Country.'

'*Uganda.*'

'Story.'

'*Lions.*'

'Rook Rifle.'

'*Farm.*'

'Shot.'

'*Suicide.*'

'Elephant.'

'*Tusks.*'

'Money.'

'*Lawyers.*'

'Thank you, Captain Black. Perhaps you could spare me a few minutes in about half an hour's time?'

'Certainly.' The young soldier looked at him curiously and wiped his brow as he got up.

'And now, Hastings,' said Poirot, smiling at me as the door closed behind him. 'You see it all, do you not?'

'I don't know what you mean.'

'Does that list of words tell you nothing?'

I scrutinized it, but was forced to shake my head.

'I will assist you. To begin with, Black answered well within the normal time limit, with no pauses, so we can take it that he himself has no guilty knowledge to conceal. "Day" to "Night" and "Place" to "Name" are normal associations. I began work with "Bernard," which might have suggested the local doctor had he come across him at all. Evidently he had not. After our recent conversation, he gave "Dinner" to my "Tuesday", but "Journey" and "Country" were answered by "Ship" and "Uganda", showing clearly that it was his journey abroad that was important to him and not the one which brought him down here. "Story" recalls to him one of the "Lion" stories he told at dinner. I proceeded to "Rook Rifle" and he answered with the totally unexpected word "Farm". When I say "Shot", he answers at once "Suicide". The association seems clear. A man he knows committed suicide with a rook rifle on a farm somewhere. Remember, too, that his mind is still on the stories he told at dinner, and I think you will agree that I shall not be far from the truth if I recall Captain Black and ask him to repeat the particular suicide story which he told at the dinner-table on Tuesday evening.'

Black was straightforward enough over the matter.

'Yes, I did tell them that story now that I come to think of it. Chap shot himself on a farm out there. Did it with a rook rifle through the roof of the mouth, bullet lodged in the brain. Doctors were no end puzzled over it – there was nothing to show except a little blood on the lips. But what –?'

'What has it got to do with Mr Maltravers? You did not know, I see, that he was found with a rook rifle by his side.'

'You mean my story suggested to him – oh, but that is awful!'

'Do not distress yourself – it would have been one way or another. Well, I must get on the telephone to London.'

Poirot had a lengthy conversation over the wire, and came back thoughtful. He went off by himself in the afternoon, and it was not till seven o'clock that he announced that he could put it off no longer, but must break the news to the young widow. My sympathy had already gone out to her unreservedly. To be left penniless, and with the knowledge that her husband had killed himself to assure her future, was a hard burden for any woman to bear. I cherished a secret hope, however, that young Black might prove capable of consoling her after her first grief had passed. He evidently admired her enormously.

Our interview with the lady was painful. She refused vehemently to believe the facts that Poirot advanced, and when she was at last convinced broke down into bitter weeping. An examination of the body turned our suspicions into certainty. Poirot was very sorry for the poor lady, but, after all, he was employed by the Insurance Company, and what could he do? As he was preparing to leave he said gently to Mrs Maltravers:

'Madame, you of all people should know that there are no dead!'

'What do you mean?' she faltered, her eyes growing wide.

'Have you never taken part in any spiritualistic séances? You are mediumistic, you know.'

'I have been told so. But you do not believe in Spiritualism, surely?'

'Madame, I have seen some strange things. You know that they say in the village that this house is haunted?'

She nodded, and at that moment the parlourmaid announced that dinner was ready.

'Won't you just stay and have something to eat?'

We accepted gracefully, and I felt that our presence could not but help distract her a little from her own griefs.

We had just finished our soup, when there was a scream outside the door, and the sound of breaking crockery. We jumped up. The parlourmaid appeared, her hand to her heart.

'It was a man – standing in the passage.'

Poirot rushed out, returning quickly.

'There is no one there.'

'Isn't there, sir?' said the parlourmaid weakly. 'Oh it did give me a start!'

'But why?'

She dropped her voice to a whisper.

'I thought – I thought it was the master – it looked like 'im.'

I saw Mrs Maltravers give a terrified start, and my mind flew to the old superstition that a suicide cannot rest. She thought of it too, I am sure, for a minute later, she caught Poirot's arm with a scream.

'Didn't you hear that? Those three taps on the window? That's how *he* always used to tap when he passed round the house.'

'The ivy,' I cried. 'It was the ivy against the pane.'

But a sort of terror was gaining on us all. The parlourmaid was obviously unstrung, and when the meal was over Mrs Maltravers besought Poirot not to go at once. She was clearly terrified to be left alone. We sat in the little morning room. The wind was getting up, and moaning round the house in an eerie fashion. Twice the door of the room came unlatched and the door slowly opened, and each time she clung to me with a terrified gasp.

'Ah, but this door, it is bewitched!' cried Poirot angrily at last. He got up and shut it once more, then turned the key in the lock. 'I shall lock it, so!'

'Don't do that,' she gasped. 'If it should come open now –'

And even as she spoke the impossible happened. The locked door slowly swung open. I could not see into the passage from where I sat, but she and Poirot were facing it. She gave one long shriek as she turned to him.

'You saw him – there in the passage?' she cried.

He was staring down at her with a puzzled face, then shook his head.

'I saw him – my husband – you must have seen him too?'

'Madame, I saw nothing. You are not well – unstrung –'

'I am perfectly well, I – Oh, God!'

Suddenly, without warning, the lights quivered and went out. Out of the darkness came three loud raps. I could hear Mrs Maltravers moaning.

And then – I saw!

The man I had seen on the bed upstairs stood there facing us, gleaming with a faint ghostly light. There was blood on his lips, and he held his right hand out, pointing. Suddenly a brilliant light seemed to proceed from it. It passed over Poirot and me, and fell on Mrs Maltravers. I saw her white terrified face, and something else!

'My God, Poirot!' I cried. 'Look at her hand, her right hand. It's all red!'

Her own eyes fell on it, and she collapsed in a heap on the floor.

'Blood,' she cried hysterically. 'Yes, it's blood. I killed him. I did it. He was showing me, and then I put my hand on the trigger and pressed. Save me from him – save me! He's come back!'

Her voice died away in a gurgle.

'Lights,' said Poirot briskly.

The lights went on as if by magic.

'That's it,' he continued. 'You heard, Hastings? And you, Everett? Oh, by the way, this is Mr Everett, rather a fine member of the theatrical profession. I phoned to him this afternoon. His make-up is good, isn't it? Quite like the dead man, and with a pocket torch and the necessary phosphorescence he made the proper impression. I shouldn't touch her right hand if I were you, Hastings. Red paint marks so. When the lights went out I clasped her hand, you see. By the way, we mustn't miss our train. Inspector Japp is outside the window. A bad night – but he has been able to while away the time by tapping on the window every now and then.'

'You see,' continued Poirot, as we walked briskly through the wind and rain, 'there was a little discrepancy. The doctor seemed to think the deceased was a Christian Scientist, and who could have given him that impression but Mrs Maltravers? But to us she represented him as being in a great state of apprehension about his own health. Again, why was she so taken aback by the reappearance of young Black? And lastly although I know that convention decrees that a woman must make a decent pretence of mourning for her husband, I do not care for such heavily-rouged eyelids! You did not observe them, Hastings? No? As I always tell you, you see nothing!

'Well, there it was. There were the two possibilities. Did Black's story suggest an ingenious method of committing suicide to Mr Maltravers, or did his other listener, the wife, see an equally ingenious method of committing murder? I inclined to the latter view. To shoot himself in the way indicated, he would probably have had to pull the trigger with his toe – or at least so I imagine. Now if Maltravers had been found with one boot off, we should almost certainly have heard of it from someone. An odd detail like that would have been remembered.

'No, as I say, I inclined to the view that it was the case of murder, not suicide, but I realized that I had not a shadow of proof in support of my theory. Hence the elaborate little comedy you saw played tonight.'

'Even now I don't quite see all the details of the crime,' I said.

'Let us start from the beginning. Here is a shrewd and scheming woman who, knowing of her husband's financial *débâcle* and tired of the elderly mate she had only married for his money, induces him to insure his life for a large sum, and then seeks for the means to accomplish her purpose. An accident gives her that – the young soldier's strange story. The next afternoon when *monsieur le capitaine*, as she thinks, is on the high seas, she and her husband are strolling round the grounds. "What a curious story that was last night!" she observes. "Could a man shoot himself in such a way? Do show me if it is possible!" The poor fool – he shows her. He places the end of his rifle in his mouth. She stoops down, and puts her finger on the trigger, laughing up at him. "And now, sir," she says saucily, "supposing I pull the trigger?"

'And then – and then, Hastings – she pulls it!'

Part 3

The Adventure of the Cheap Flat

So far, in the cases which I have recorded, Poirot's investigations have started from the central fact, whether murder or robbery, and have proceeded from thence by a process of logical deduction to the final triumphant unravelling. In the events I am now about to chronicle a remarkable chain of circumstances led from the apparently trivial incidents which first attracted Poirot's attention to the sinister happenings which completed a most unusual case.

I had been spending the evening with an old friend of mine, Gerald Parker. There had been, perhaps, about half a dozen people there besides my host and myself, and the talk fell, as it was bound to do sooner or later wherever Parker found himself, on the subject of house-hunting in London. Houses and flats were Parker's special hobby. Since the end of the War, he had occupied at least half a dozen different flats and maisonettes. No sooner was he settled anywhere than he would light unexpectedly upon a new find, and would forthwith depart bag and baggage. His moves were nearly always accomplished at a slight pecuniary gain, for he had a shrewd business head, but it was sheer love of the sport that actuated him, and not a desire to make money at it. We listened to Parker for some time with the respect of the novice for the expert. Then it was our turn, and a perfect babel of tongues was let loose. Finally the floor was left to Mrs Robinson, a charming little bride who was there with her husband. I had never met them before, as Robinson was only a recent acquaintance of Parker's.

'Talking of flats,' she said, 'have you heard of our piece of luck, Mr Parker? We've got a flat – at last! In Montagu Mansions.'

'Well,' said Parker, 'I've always said there are plenty of flats – at a price!'

'Yes, but this isn't at a price. It's dirt cheap. Eighty pounds a year!'

'But – but Montagu Mansions is just off Knightsbridge, isn't it? Big handsome building. Or are you talking of a poor relation of the same name stuck in the slums somewhere?'

'No, it's the Knightsbridge one. That's what makes it so wonderful.'

'Wonderful is the word! It's a blinking miracle. But

66

there must be a catch somewhere. Big premium, I suppose?'

'No premium!'

'No prem – oh, hold my head, somebody!' groaned Parker.

'But we've got to buy the furniture,' continued Mrs Robinson.

'Ah!' Parker bristled up. 'I knew there was a catch!'

'For fifty pounds. And it's beautifully furnished!'

'I give it up,' said Parker. 'The present occupants must be lunatics with a taste for philanthropy.'

Mrs Robinson was looking a little troubled. A little pucker appeared between her dainty brows.

'It *is* queer, isn't it? You don't think that – that – the place is *haunted*?'

'Never heard of a haunted flat,' declared Parker decisively.

'No-o.' Mrs Robinson appeared far from convinced. 'But there were several things about it all that struck me as – well, queer.'

'For instance –' I suggested.

'Ah,' said Parker, 'our criminal expert's attention is aroused! Unburden yourself to him, Mrs Robinson. Hastings is a great unraveller of mysteries.'

I laughed, embarrassed, but not wholly displeased with the rôle thrust upon me.

'Oh, not really queer, Captain Hastings, but when

we went to the agents, Stosser and Paul – we hadn't
tried them before because they only have the expensive
Mayfair flats, but we thought at any rate it would do
no harm – everything they offered us was four and five
hundred a year, or else huge premiums, and then, just
as we were going, they mentioned that they had a flat
at eighty, but that they doubted if it would be any good
our going there, because it had been on their books
some time and they had sent so many people to see it
that it was almost sure to be taken – "snapped up" as
the clerk put it – only people were so tiresome in not
letting them know, and then they went on sending, and
people get annoyed at being sent to a place that had,
perhaps, been let some time.'

Mrs Robinson paused for some much needed breath,
and then continued:

'We thanked him, and said that we quite understood
it would probably be no good, but that we should like
an order all the same – just in case. And we went there
straight away in a taxi, for, after all, you never know.
No 4 was on the second floor, and just as we were
waiting for the lift, Elsie Ferguson – she's a friend of
mine, Captain Hastings, and they are looking for a flat
too – came hurrying down the stairs. "Ahead of you
for once, my dear," she said. "But it's no good. It's
already let." That seemed to finish it, but – well, as
John said, the place was very cheap, we could afford

to give more, and perhaps if we offered a premium. A horrid thing to do, of course, and I feel quite ashamed of telling you, but you know what flat-hunting is.'

I assured her that I was well aware that in the struggle for house-room the baser side of human nature frequently triumphed over the higher, and that the well-known rule of dog eat dog always applied.

'So we went up and, would you believe it, the flat wasn't let at all. We were shown over it by the maid, and then we saw the mistress, and the thing was settled then and there. Immediate possession and fifty pounds for the furniture. We signed the agreement next day, and we are to move in tomorrow!' Mrs Robinson paused triumphantly.

'And what about Mrs Ferguson?' asked Parker. 'Let's have your deductions, Hastings.'

'"Obvious, my dear Watson,"' I quoted lightly. 'She went to the wrong flat.'

'Oh, Captain Hastings, how clever of you!' cried Mrs Robinson admiringly.

I rather wished Poirot had been there. Sometimes I have the feeling that he rather underestimates my capabilities.

II

The whole thing was rather amusing, and I propounded the thing as a mock problem to Poirot on the following morning. He seemed interested, and questioned me rather narrowly as to the rents of flats in various localities.

'A curious story,' he said thoughtfully. 'Excuse me, Hastings, I must take a short stroll.'

When he returned, about an hour later, his eyes were gleaming with a peculiar excitement. He laid his stick on the table, and brushed the nap of his hat with his usual tender care before he spoke.

'It is as well, *mon ami*, that we have no affairs of moment on hand. We can devote ourselves wholly to the present investigation.'

'What investigation are you talking about?'

'The remarkable cheapness of your friend, Mrs Robinson's, new flat.'

'Poirot, you are not serious!'

'I am most serious. Figure to yourself, my friend, that the real rent of those flats is £350. I have just ascertained that from the landlord's agents. And yet this particular flat is being sublet at eighty pounds! Why?'

'There must be something wrong with it. Perhaps it is haunted, as Mrs Robinson suggested.'

Poirot shook his head in a dissatisfied manner.

'Then again how curious it is that her friend tells her the flat is let, and, when she goes up, behold, it is not so at all!'

'But surely you agree with me that the other woman must have gone to the wrong flat. That is the only possible solution.'

'You may or may not be right on that point, Hastings. The fact still remains that numerous other applicants were sent to see it, and yet, in spite of its remarkable cheapness, it was still in the market when Mrs Robinson arrived.'

'That shows that there *must* be something wrong about it.'

'Mrs Robinson did not seem to notice anything amiss. Very curious, is it not? Did she impress you as being a truthful woman, Hastings?'

'She was a delightful creature!'

'*Evidemment*! since she renders you incapable of replying to my question. Describe her to me, then.'

'Well, she's tall and fair; her hair's really a beautiful shade of auburn –'

'Always you have had a penchant for auburn hair!' murmured Poirot. 'But continue.'

'Blue eyes and a very nice complexion and – well, that's all, I think,' I concluded lamely.

'And her husband?'

'Oh, he's quite a nice fellow – nothing startling.'

'Dark or fair?'

'I don't know – betwixt and between, and just an ordinary sort of face.'

Poirot nodded.

'Yes, there are hundreds of these average men – and anyway, you bring more sympathy and appreciation to your description of women. Do you know anything about these people? Does Parker know them well?'

'They are just recent acquaintances, I believe. But surely, Poirot, you don't think for an instant –'

Poirot raised his hand.

'*Tout doucement, mon ami.* Have I said that I think anything? All I say is – it is a curious story. And there is nothing to throw light upon it; except perhaps the lady's name, eh, Hastings?'

'Her name is Stella,' I said stiffly, 'but I don't see –'

Poirot interrupted me with a tremendous chuckle. Something seemed to be amusing him vastly.

'And Stella means a star, does it not? Famous!'

'What on earth –?'

'And stars give light! *Voilà*! Calm yourself, Hastings. Do not put on that air of injured dignity. Come, we will go to Montagu Mansions and make a few inquiries.'

I accompanied him, nothing loath. The Mansions were a handsome block of buildings in excellent repair.

A uniformed porter was sunning himself on the threshold, and it was to him that Poirot addressed himself.

'Pardon, but would you tell me if a Mr and Mrs Robinson reside here?'

The porter was a man of few words and apparently of a sour or suspicious disposition. He hardly looked at us and grunted out:

'No 4. Second floor.'

'I thank you. Can you tell me how long they have been here?'

'Six months.'

I started forward in amazement, conscious as I did so of Poirot's malicious grin.

'Impossible,' I cried. 'You must be making a mistake.'

'Six months.'

'Are you sure? The lady I mean is tall and fair with reddish gold hair and –'

'That's 'er,' said the porter. 'Come in the Michaelmas quarter, they did. Just six months ago.'

He appeared to lose interest in us and retreated slowly up the hall. I followed Poirot outside.

'*Eh bien*, Hastings?' my friend demanded slyly. 'Are you so sure now that delightful women always speak the truth?'

I did not reply.

Poirot had steered his way into Brompton Road before I asked him what he was going to do and where we were going.

'To the house agents, Hastings. I have a great desire to have a flat in Montagu Mansions. If I am not mistaken, several interesting things will take place there before long.'

We were fortunate in our quest. No 8, on the fourth floor, was to be let furnished at ten guineas a week, Poirot promptly took it for a month. Outside in the street again, he silenced my protests:

'But I make money nowadays! Why should I not indulge a whim? By the way, Hastings, have you a revolver?'

'Yes – somewhere,' I answered, slightly thrilled. 'Do you think –'

'That you will need it? It is quite possible. The idea pleases you, I see. Always the spectacular and romantic appeals to you.'

The following day saw us installed in our temporary home. The flat was pleasantly furnished. It occupied the same position in the building as that of the Robinsons, but was two floors higher.

The day after our installation was a Sunday. In the afternoon, Poirot left the front door ajar, and summoned me hastily as a bang reverberated from somewhere below.

'Look over the banisters. Are those your friends? Do not let them see you.'

I craned my neck over the staircase.

'That's them,' I declared in an ungrammatical whisper.

'Good. Wait awhile.'

About half an hour later, a young woman emerged in brilliant and varied clothing. With a sigh of satisfaction, Poirot tiptoed back into the flat.

'*C'est ça*. After the master and mistress, the maid. The flat should now be empty.'

'What are we going to do?' I asked uneasily.

Poirot had trotted briskly into the scullery and was hauling at the rope of the coal-lift.

'We are about to descend after the method of the dustbins,' he explained cheerfully. 'No one will observe us. The Sunday concert, the Sunday "afternoon out", and finally the Sunday nap after the Sunday dinner of England – *le rosbif* – all these will distract attention from the doings of Hercule Poirot. Come, my friend.'

He stepped into the rough wooden contrivance and I followed him gingerly.

'Are we going to break into the flat?' I asked dubiously.

Poirot's answer was not too reassuring:

'Not precisely today,' he replied.

Pulling on the rope, we descended slowly till we

75

reached the second floor. Poirot uttered an exclamation of satisfaction as he perceived that the wooden door into the scullery was open.

'You observe? Never do they bolt these doors in the daytime. And yet anyone could mount or descend as we have done. At night, yes – though not always then – and it is against that that we are going to make provision.'

He had drawn some tools from his pocket as he spoke, and at once set deftly to work, his object being to arrange the bolt so that it could be pulled back from the lift. The operation only occupied about three minutes. Then Poirot returned the tools to his pocket, and we reascended once more to our own domain.

III

On Monday Poirot was out all day, but when he returned in the evening he flung himself into his chair with a sigh of satisfaction.

'Hastings, shall I recount to you a little history? A story after your own heart and which will remind you of your favourite cinema?'

'Go ahead,' I laughed. 'I presume that it is a true story, not one of your efforts of fancy.'

'It is true enough. Inspector Japp of Scotland Yard will vouch for its accuracy, since it was through his kind offices that it came to my ears. Listen, Hastings. A little over six months ago some important Naval plans were stolen from an American Government department. They showed the position of some of the most important Harbour defences, and would be worth a considerable sum to any foreign Government – that of Japan, for example. Suspicion fell upon a young man named Luigi Valdarno, an Italian by birth, who was employed in a minor capacity in the Department and who was missing at the same time as the papers. Whether Luigi Valdarno was the thief or not, he was found two days later on the East Side in New York, shot dead. The papers were not on him. Now for some time past Luigi Valdarno had been going about with a Miss Elsa Hardt, a young concert singer who had recently appeared and who lived with a brother in an apartment in Washington. Nothing was known of the antecedents of Miss Elsa Hardt, and she disappeared suddenly about the time of Valdarno's death. There are reasons for believing that she was in reality an accomplished international spy who has done much nefarious work under various aliases. The American Secret Service, while doing their best to trace her, also kept an eye upon certain insignificant Japanese gentlemen living in Washington. They felt pretty certain that, when Elsa Hardt had covered her tracks sufficiently, she would approach the gentlemen in question. One of them left suddenly for England a fortnight ago. On the face of it, therefore, it would seem that Elsa Hardt is in England.' Poirot paused, and then added softly: 'The official description of Elsa Hardt is: Height 5 ft 7, eyes blue, hair auburn, fair complexion, nose straight, no special distinguishing marks.'

'Mrs Robinson!' I gasped.

'Well, there is a chance of it, anyhow,' amended Poirot. 'Also I learn that a swarthy man, a foreigner of some kind, was inquiring about the occupants of No 4 only this morning. Therefore, *mon ami*, I fear that you must forswear your beauty sleep tonight, and join me in my all-night vigil in that flat below – armed with that excellent revolver of yours, *bien entendu!*'

'Rather,' I cried with enthusiasm. 'When shall we start?'

'The hour of midnight is both solemn and suitable, I fancy. Nothing is likely to occur before then.'

At twelve o'clock precisely, we crept cautiously into the coal-lift and lowered ourselves to the second floor. Under Poirot's manipulation, the wooden door quickly swung inwards, and we climbed into the flat. From the scullery we passed into the kitchen where we established ourselves comfortably in two chairs with the door into the hall ajar.

'Now we have but to wait,' said Poirot contentedly, closing his eyes.

To me, the waiting appeared endless. I was terrified of going to sleep. Just when it seemed to me that I had been there about eight hours – and had, as I found out afterwards, in reality been exactly one hour and twenty minutes – a faint scratching sound came to my ears. Poirot's hand touched mine. I rose, and together we moved carefully in the direction of the hall. The noise came from there. Poirot placed his lips to my ear.

'Outside the front door. They are cutting out the lock. When I give the word, not before, fall upon him from behind and hold him fast. Be careful, he will have a knife.'

Presently there was a rending sound, and a little circle of light appeared through the door. It was extinguished immediately and then the door was slowly opened. Poirot and I flattened ourselves against the wall. I heard a man's breathing as he passed us. Then he flashed on his torch, and as he did so, Poirot hissed in my ear:

'*Allez.*'

We sprang together, Poirot with a quick movement enveloped the intruder's head with a light woollen scarf whilst I pinioned his arms. The whole affair was quick and noiseless. I twisted a dagger from his hand, and as Poirot brought down the scarf from his eyes, whilst keeping it wound tightly round his mouth, I jerked up my revolver where he could see it and understand that resistance was useless. As he ceased to struggle Poirot put his mouth close to his ear and began to whisper rapidly. After a minute the man nodded. Then enjoining silence with a movement of the hand, Poirot led the way out of the flat and down the stairs. Our captive followed, and I brought up the rear with the revolver. When we were out in the street, Poirot turned to me.

'There is a taxi waiting just round the corner. Give me the revolver. We shall not need it now.'

'But if this fellow tries to escape?'

Poirot smiled.

'He will not.'

I returned in a minute with the waiting taxi. The scarf had been unwound from the stranger's face, and I gave a start of surprise.

'He's not a Jap,' I ejaculated in a whisper to Poirot.

'Observation was always your strong point, Hastings! Nothing escapes you. No, the man is not a Jap. He is an Italian.'

We got into the taxi, and Poirot gave the driver an address in St John's Wood. I was by now completely fogged. I did not like to ask Poirot where we were going in front of our captive, and strove in vain to obtain some light upon the proceedings.

We alighted at the door of a small house standing back from the road. A returning wayfarer, slightly drunk, was lurching along the pavement and almost collided with Poirot, who said something sharply to him which I did not catch. All three of us went up the steps of the house. Poirot rang the bell and motioned us to stand a little aside. There was no answer and he rang again and then seized the knocker which he plied for some minutes vigorously.

A light appeared suddenly above the fanlight, and the door opened cautiously a little way.

'What the devil do you want?' a man's voice demanded harshly.

'I want the doctor. My wife is taken ill.'

'There's no doctor here.'

The man prepared to shut the door, but Poirot thrust his foot in adroitly. He became suddenly a perfect caricature of an infuriated Frenchman.

'What you say, there is no doctor? I will have the law of you. You must come! I will stay here and ring and knock all night.'

'My dear sir –' The door was opened again, the man, clad in a dressing-gown and slippers, stepped forward to pacify Poirot with an uneasy glance round.

'I will call the police.'

Poirot prepared to descend the steps.

'No, don't do that for Heaven's sake!' The man dashed after him.

With a neat push Poirot sent him staggering down

Agatha Christie

the steps. In another minute all three of us were inside the door and it was pushed to and bolted.

'Quick – in here.' Poirot led the way into the nearest room, switching on the light as he did so. 'And you – behind the curtain.'

'Si, Signor,' said the Italian and slid rapidly behind the full folds of rose-coloured velvet which draped the embrasure of the window.

Not a minute too soon. Just as he disappeared from view a woman rushed into the room. She was tall with reddish hair and held a scarlet kimono round her slender form.

'Where is my husband?' she cried, with a quick frightened glance. 'Who are you?'

Poirot stepped forward with a bow.

'It is to be hoped your husband will not suffer from a chill. I observed that he had slippers on his feet, and that his dressing-gown was a warm one.'

'Who are you? What are you doing in my house?'

'It is true that none of us have the pleasure of your acquaintance, madame. It is especially to be regretted as one of our number has come specially from New York in order to meet you.'

The curtains parted and the Italian stepped out. To my horror I observed that he was brandishing my revolver, which Poirot must doubtless have put down through inadvertence in the cab.

The woman gave a piercing scream and turned to fly, but Poirot was standing in front of the closed door.

'Let me by,' she shrieked. 'He will murder me.'

'Who was it dat croaked Luigi Valdarno?' asked the Italian hoarsely, brandishing the weapon, and sweeping each one of us with it. We dared not move.

'My God, Poirot, this is awful. What shall we do?' I cried.

'You will oblige me by refraining from talking so much, Hastings. I can assure you that our friend will not shoot until I give the word.'

'Youse sure o' dat, eh?' said the Italian, leering unpleasantly.

It was more than I was, but the woman turned to Poirot like a flash.

'What is it you want?'

Poirot bowed.

'I do not think it is necessary to insult Miss Elsa Hardt's intelligence by telling her.'

With a swift movement, the woman snatched up a big black velvet cat which served as a cover for the telephone.

'They are stitched in the lining of that.'

'Clever,' murmured Poirot appreciatively. He stood aside from the door. 'Good evening, madame. I will detain your friend from New York whilst you make your getaway.'

Agatha Christie

'Whatta fool!' roared the big Italian, and raising the revolver he fired point-blank at the woman's retreating figure just as I flung myself upon him.

But the weapon merely clicked harmlessly and Poirot's voice rose in mild reproof.

'Never will you trust your old friend, Hastings. I do not care for my friends to carry loaded pistols about with them and never would I permit a mere acquaintance to do so. No, no, *mon ami*.' This to the Italian who was swearing hoarsely. Poirot continued to address him in a tone of mild reproof: 'See now, what I have done for you. I have saved you from being hanged. And do not think that our beautiful lady will escape. No, no, the house is watched, back and front. Straight into the arms of the police they will go. Is not that a beautiful and consoling thought? Yes, you may leave the room now. But be careful – be very careful. I – Ah, he is gone! And my friend Hastings looks at me with eyes of reproach. But it's all so simple! It was clear, from the first, that out of several hundred, probably, applicants for No 4 Montagu Mansions, only the Robinsons were considered suitable. Why? What was there that singled them out from the rest – at practically a glance. Their appearance? Possibly, but it was not so unusual. Their name, then!'

'But there's nothing unusual about the name of Robinson,' I cried. 'It's quite a common name.'

'Ah! *Sapristi*, but exactly! That was the point. Elsa Hardt and her husband, or brother or whatever he really is, come from New York, and take a flat in the name of Mr and Mrs Robinson. Suddenly they learn that one of these secret societies, the Mafia, or the Camorra, to which doubtless Luigi Valdarno belonged, is on their track. What do they do? They hit on a scheme of transparent simplicity. Evidently they knew that their pursuers were not personally acquainted with either of them. What, then, can be simpler? They offer the flat at an absurdly low rental. Of the thousands of young couples in London looking for flats, there cannot fail to be several Robinsons. It is only a matter of waiting. If you will look at the name of Robinson in the telephone directory, you will realize that a fair-haired Mrs Robinson was pretty sure to come along sooner or later. Then what will happen? The avenger arrives. He knows the name, he knows the address. He strikes! All is over, vengeance is satisfied, and Miss Elsa Hardt has escaped by the skin of her teeth once more. By the way, Hastings, you must present me to the real Mrs Robinson – that delightful and truthful creature! What will they think when they find their flat has been broken into! We must hurry back. Ah, that sounds like Japp and his friends arriving.'

A mighty tattoo sounded on the knocker.

'How do you know this address?' I asked as I followed Poirot out into the hall. 'Oh, of course, you had the first Mrs Robinson followed when she left the other flat.'

'*A la bonne heure*, Hastings. You use your grey cells at last. Now for a little surprise for Japp.'

Softly unbolting the door, he stuck the cat's head round the edge and ejaculated a piercing 'Miaow'.

The Scotland Yard inspector, who was standing outside with another man, jumped in spite of himself.

'Oh, it's only Monsieur Poirot at one of his little jokes!' he exclaimed, as Poirot's head followed that of the cat. 'Let us in, moosior.'

'You have our friends safe and sound?'

'Yes, we've got the birds all right. But they hadn't got the goods with them.'

'I see. So you come to search. Well, I am about to depart with Hastings, but I should like to give you a little lecture upon the history and habits of the domestic cat.'

'For the Lord's sake, have you gone completely balmy?'

'The cat,' declaimed Poirot, 'was worshipped by the ancient Egyptians. It is still regarded as a symbol of good luck if a black cat crosses your path. This cat crossed your path tonight, Japp. To speak of the interior of any animal or any person is not. I know, considered polite in England. But the interior of this cat is perfectly delicate. I refer to the lining.'

With a sudden grunt, the second man seized the cat from Poirot's hand.

'Oh, I forgot to introduce you,' said Japp. 'Mr Poirot, this is Mr Burt of the United States Secret Service.'

The American's trained fingers had felt what he was looking for. He held out his hand, and for a moment speech failed him. Then he rose to the occasion.

'Pleased to meet you,' said Mr Burt.

Part 4

The Mystery of Hunter's Lodge

'After all,' murmured Poirot, 'it is possible that I shall not die this time.'

Coming from a convalescent influenza patient, I hailed the remark as showing a beneficial optimism. I myself had been the first sufferer from the disease. Poirot in his turn had gone down. He was now sitting up in bed, propped up with pillows, his head muffled in a woollen shawl, and was slowly sipping a particularly noxious *tisane* which I had prepared according to his directions. His eye rested with pleasure upon a neatly graduated row of medicine bottles which adorned the mantelpiece.

'Yes, yes,' my little friend continued. 'Once more shall I be myself again, the great Hercule Poirot, the terror of evildoers! Figure to yourself, *mon ami*, that I have a little paragraph to myself in *Society Gossip*. But yes! Here it is: "Go it – criminals – all out!

Hercule Poirot – and believe me, girls, he's some Hercules! – our own pet society detective can't get a grip on you. 'Cause why? 'Cause he's got *la grippe* himself"'!'

I laughed.

'Good for you, Poirot. You are becoming quite a public character. And fortunately you haven't missed anything of particular interest during this time.'

'That is true. The few cases I have had to decline did not fill me with any regret.'

Our landlady stuck her head in at the door.

'There's a gentleman downstairs. Says he must see Monsieur Poirot or you, Captain. Seeing as he was in a great to-do – and with all that quite the gentleman – I brought up 'is card.'

She handed me a bit of pasteboard. 'Mr Roger Havering,' I read.

Poirot motioned with his head towards the bookcase, and I obediently pulled forth *Who's Who*. Poirot took it from me and scanned the pages rapidly.

'Second son of fifth Baron Windsor. Married 1913 Zoe, fourth daughter of William Crabb.'

'H'm!' I said. 'I rather fancy that's the girl who used to act at the Frivolity – only she called herself Zoe Carrisbrook. I remember she married some young man about town just before the War.'

'Would it interest you, Hastings, to go down and hear

what our visitor's particular little trouble is? Make him all my excuses.'

Roger Havering was a man of about forty, well set up and of smart appearance. His face, however, was haggard, and he was evidently labouring under great agitation.

'Captain Hastings? You are Monsieur Poirot's partner, I understand. It is imperative that he should come with me to Derbyshire today.'

'I'm afraid that's impossible,' I replied. 'Poirot is ill in bed – influenza.'

His face fell.

'Dear me, that is a great blow to me.'

'The matter on which you want to consult him is serious?'

'My God, yes! My uncle, the best friend I have in the world, was foully murdered last night.'

'Here in London?'

'No, in Derbyshire. I was in town and received a telegram from my wife this morning. Immediately upon its receipt I determined to come round and beg Monsieur Poirot to undertake the case.'

'If you will excuse me a minute,' I said, struck by a sudden idea.

I rushed upstairs, and in a few brief words acquainted Poirot with the situation. He took any further words out of my mouth.

'I see. I see. You want to go yourself, is it not so? Well, why not? You should know my methods by now. All I ask is that you should report to me fully every day, and follow implicitly any instructions I may wire you.'

To this I willingly agreed.

II

An hour later I was sitting opposite Mr Havering in a first-class carriage on the Midland Railway, speeding rapidly away from London.

'To begin with, Captain Hastings, you must understand that Hunter's Lodge, where we are going, and where the tragedy took place, is only a small shooting-box in the heart of the Derbyshire moors. Our real home is near Newmarket, and we usually rent a flat in town for the season. Hunter's Lodge is looked after by a housekeeper who is quite capable of doing all we need when we run down for an occasional weekend. Of course, during the shooting season, we take down some of our own servants from Newmarket. My uncle, Mr Harrington Pace (as you may know, my mother was a Miss Pace of New York), has, for the last three years, made his home with us. He never got on well with my father, or my elder brother, and I suspect that my being somewhat of a prodigal son myself rather increased than diminished his affection towards me. Of course I am a poor man, and my uncle was a rich one – in other words, he paid the piper! But, though exacting in many ways, he was not really hard to get on with, and we all three lived very harmoniously together. Two days ago, my uncle, rather wearied with some recent gaieties of ours in town, suggested that we should run down to Derbyshire for a day or two. My wife telegraphed to Mrs Middleton, the housekeeper, and we went down that same afternoon. Yesterday evening I was forced to return to town, but my wife and my uncle remained on. This morning I received this telegram.' He handed it over to me:

'Come at once uncle Harrington murdered last night bring good detective if you can but do come – Zoe.'

'Then, as yet you know no details?'

'No, I suppose it will be in the evening papers. Without doubt the police are in charge.'

It was about three o'clock when we arrived at the little station of Elmer's Dale. From there a five-mile drive brought us to a small grey stone building in the midst of the rugged moors.

'A lonely place,' I observed with a shiver.

Havering nodded.

'I shall try and get rid of it. I could never live here again.'

We unlatched the gate and were walking up the narrow path to the oak door when a familiar figure emerged and came to meet us.

'Japp!' I ejaculated.

The Scotland Yard inspector grinned at me in a friendly fashion before addressing my companion.

'Mr Havering, I think? I've been sent down from London to take charge of this case, and I'd like a word with you, if I may, sir.'

'My wife –'

'I've seen your good lady, sir – and the housekeeper. I won't keep you a moment, but I am anxious to get back to the village now that I've seen all there is to see here.'

'I know nothing as yet as to what –'

'Ex-actly,' said Japp soothingly. 'But there are just one or two little points I'd like your opinion about all the same. Captain Hastings here, he knows me, and he'll go on up to the house and tell them you're coming. What have you done with the little man, by the way, Captain Hastings?'

'He's ill in bed with influenza.'

'Is he now? I'm sorry to hear that. Rather the case of the cart without the horse, you being here without him, isn't it?'

And on his rather ill-timed jest I went on to the house. I rang the bell, as Japp had closed the door behind him. After some moments it was opened to me by a middle-aged woman in black.

'Mr Havering will be here in a moment,' I explained. 'He has been detained by the inspector. I have come down with him from London to look into the case. Perhaps you can tell me briefly what occurred last night.'

'Come inside, sir.' She closed the door behind me, and we stood in the dimly-lighted hall. 'It was after dinner last night, sir, that the man came. He asked to see Mr Pace, sir, and, seeing that he spoke the same way, I thought it was an American gentleman friend of Mr Pace's and I showed him into the gun-room, and then went to tell Mr Pace. He wouldn't give any name, which, of course, was a bit odd, now I come to think of it. I told Mr Pace, and he seemed puzzled like, but he said to the mistress: "Excuse me, Zoe, while I see what this fellow wants." He went off to the gun-room, and I went back to the kitchen, but after a while I heard loud voices, as if they were quarrelling, and I came out into the hall. At the same time, the mistress she comes out too, and just then there was a shot and then a dreadful silence. We both ran to the gun-room door, but it was locked and we had to go round to the window. It was open, and there inside was Mr Pace, all shot and bleeding.'

'What became of the man?'

'He must have got away through the window, sir, before we got to it.'

'And then?'

'Mrs Havering sent me to fetch the police. Five miles to walk it was. They came back with me, and the constable he stayed all night, and this morning the police gentleman from London arrived.'

'What was this man like who called to see Mr Pace?'

The housekeeper reflected.

'He had a black beard, sir, and was about middle-aged, and had on a light overcoat. Beyond the fact that he spoke like an American I didn't notice much about him.'

'I see. Now I wonder if I can see Mrs Havering?'

'She's upstairs, sir. Shall I tell her?'

'If you please. Tell her that Mr Havering is outside with Inspector Japp, and that the gentleman he has brought back with him from London is anxious to speak to her as soon as possible.'

'Very good, sir.'

I was in a fever of impatience to get all the facts. Japp had two or three hours' start on me, and his anxiety to be gone made me keen to be close at his heels.

Mrs Havering did not keep me waiting long. In a few minutes I heard a light step descending the stairs, and looked up to see a very handsome young woman coming towards me. She wore a flame-coloured jumper, that set off the slender boyishness of her figure. On her dark head was a little hat of flame-coloured leather. Even the present tragedy could not dim the vitality of her personality.

I introduced myself, and she nodded in quick comprehension.

'Of course I have often heard of you and your colleague, Monsieur Poirot. You have done some wonderful things together, haven't you? It was very clever of my husband to get you so promptly. Now will you ask me questions? That is the easiest way, isn't it, of getting to know all you want to about this dreadful affair?'

'Thank you, Mrs Havering. Now what time was it that this man arrived?'

'It must have been just before nine o'clock. We had finished dinner, and were sitting over our coffee and cigarettes.'

'Your husband had already left for London?'

'Yes, he went up by the 6.15.'

'Did he go by car to the station, or did he walk?'

'Our own car isn't down here. One came out from the garage in Elmer's Dale to fetch him in time for the train.'

'Was Mr Pace quite his usual self?'

97

'Absolutely. Most normal in every way.'

'Now, can you describe this visitor at all?'

'I'm afraid not. I didn't see him. Mrs Middleton showed him straight into the gun-room and then came to tell my uncle.'

'What did your uncle say?'

'He seemed rather annoyed, but went off at once. It was about five minutes later that I heard the sound of raised voices. I ran out into the hall and almost collided with Mrs Middleton. Then we heard the shot. The gun-room door was locked on the inside, and we had to go right round the house to the window. Of course that took some time, and the murderer had been able to get well away. My poor uncle' – her voice faltered – 'had been shot through the head. I saw at once that he was dead. I sent Mrs Middleton for the police, I was careful to touch nothing in the room but to leave it exactly as I found it.'

I nodded approval.

'Now, as to the weapon?'

'Well, I can make a guess at it, Captain Hastings. A pair of revolvers of my husband's were mounted upon the wall. One of them is missing. I pointed this out to the police, and they took the other one away with them. When they have extracted the bullet, I suppose they will know for certain.'

'May I go to the gun-room?'

'Certainly. The police have finished with it. But the body has been removed.'

She accompanied me to the scene of the crime. At that moment Havering entered the hall, and with a quick apology his wife ran to him. I was left to undertake my investigations alone.

I may as well confess at once that they were rather disappointing. In detective novels clues abound, but here I could find nothing that struck me as out of the ordinary except a large blood-stain on the carpet where I judged the dead man had fallen. I examined everything with painstaking care and took a couple of pictures of the room with my little camera which I had brought with me. I also examined the ground outside the window, but it appeared to have been so heavily trampled underfoot that I judged it was useless to waste time over it. No, I had seen all that Hunter's Lodge had to show me. I must go back to Elmer's Dale and get into touch with Japp. Accordingly I took leave of the Haverings, and was driven off in the car that had brought us from the station.

I found Japp at the Matlock Arms and he took me forthwith to see the body. Harrington Pace was a small, spare, clean-shaven man, typically American in appearance. He had been shot through the back of the head, and the revolver had been discharged at close quarters.

Agatha Christie

'Turned away for a moment,' remarked Japp, 'and the other fellow snatched up a revolver and shot him. The one Mrs Havering handed over to us was fully loaded and I suppose the other one was also. Curious what darn fool things people do. Fancy keeping two loaded revolvers hanging up on your wall.'

'What do you think of the case?' I asked, as we left the gruesome chamber behind us.

'Well, I'd got my eye on Havering to begin with. Oh, yes!' – noting my exclamation of astonishment. 'Havering has one or two shady incidents in his past. When he was a boy at Oxford there was some funny business about the signature on one of his father's cheques. All hushed up of course. Then, he's pretty heavily in debt now, and they're the kind of debts he wouldn't like to go to his uncle about, whereas you may be sure the uncle's will would be in his favour. Yes, I'd got my eye on him, and that's why I wanted to speak to him before he saw his wife, but their statements dovetail all right, and I've been to the station and there's no doubt whatever that he left by the 6.15. That gets up to London about 10.30. He went straight to his club, he says, and if that's confirmed all right – why, he couldn't have been shooting his uncle here at nine o'clock in a black beard!'

'Ah, yes, I was going to ask you what you thought about that beard?'

Japp winked.

'I think it grew pretty fast – grew in the five miles from Elmer's Dale to Hunter's Lodge. Americans that I've met are mostly clean-shaven. Yes, it's amongst Mr Pace's American associates that we'll have to look for the murderer. I questioned the housekeeper first, and then her mistress, and their stories agree all right, but I'm sorry Mrs Havering didn't get a look at the fellow. She's a smart woman, and she might have noticed something that would set us on the track.'

I sat down and wrote a minute and lengthy account to Poirot. I was able to add various further items of information before I posted the letter.

The bullet had been extracted and was proved to have been fired from a revolver identical with the one held by the police. Furthermore, Mr Havering's movements on the night in question had been checked and verified, and it was proved beyond doubt that he had actually arrived in London by the train in question. And, thirdly, a sensational development had occurred. A city gentleman, living at Ealing, on crossing Haven Green to get to the District Railway Station that morning, had observed a brown-paper parcel stuck between the railings. Opening it, he found that it contained a revolver. He handed the parcel over to the local police station, and before night it was proved to be the one we were in search of, the fellow to that given us by Mrs Havering. One bullet had been fired from it.

All this I added to my report. A wire from Poirot arrived whilst I was at breakfast the following morning:

> 'Of course black-bearded man was not Havering only you or Japp would have such an idea wire me description of housekeeper and what clothes she wore this morning same of Mrs Havering do not waste time taking photographs of interiors they are underexposed and not in the least artistic.'

It seemed to me that Poirot's style was unnecessarily facetious. I also fancied he was a shade jealous of my position on the spot with full facilities for handling the case. His request for a description of the clothes worn by the two women appeared to me to be simply ridiculous, but I complied as well as I, a mere man, was able to.

At eleven a reply wire came from Poirot:

> 'Advise Japp arrest housekeeper before it is too late.'

Dumbfounded, I took the wire to Japp. He swore softly under his breath.

'He's the goods, Monsieur Poirot: if he says so, there's something in it. And I hardly noticed the woman. I don't know that I can go so far as arresting her, but I'll have her watched. We'll go up right away, and take another look at her.'

But it was too late, Mrs Middleton, that quiet middle-aged woman, who had appeared so normal and respectable, had vanished into thin air. Her box had been left behind. It contained only ordinary wearing apparel. There was no clue to her identity, or as to her whereabouts.

From Mrs Havering we elicited all the facts we could:

'I engaged her about three weeks ago when Mrs Emery, our former housekeeper, left. She came to me from Mrs Selbourne's Agency in Mount Street – a very well-known place. I get all my servants from there. They sent several women to see me, but this Mrs Middleton seemed much the nicest, and had splendid references. I engaged her on the spot, and notified the Agency of the fact. I can't believe that there was anything wrong with her. She was such a nice quiet woman.'

The thing was certainly a mystery. Whilst it was clear that the woman herself could not have committed the crime, since at the moment the shot was fired Mrs Havering was with her in the hall, nevertheless she must have some connection with the murder, or why should she suddenly take to her heels and bolt?

I wired the latest development to Poirot and suggested returning to London and making inquiries at Selbourne's Agency.

Poirot's reply was prompt:

'Useless to inquire at agency they will never have heard of her find out what vehicle took her up to hunters lodge when she first arrived there.'

Though mystified, I was obedient. The means of transport in Elmer's Dale were limited. The local garage had two battered Ford cars, and there were two station flies. None of these had been requisitioned on the date in question. Questioned, Mrs Havering explained that she had given the woman the money for her fare down to Derbyshire and sufficient to hire a car or fly to take her up to Hunter's Lodge. There was usually one of the Fords at the station on the chance of its being required. Taking into consideration the further fact that nobody at the station had noticed the arrival of a stranger, black-bearded or otherwise, on the fatal evening, everything seemed to point to the conclusion that the murderer had come to the spot in a car, which had been waiting near at hand to aid his escape, and that the same car had brought the mysterious housekeeper to her new post. I may mention that inquiries at the Agency in London bore out Poirot's prognostication. No such woman as 'Mrs Middleton' had ever been on their books. They had received the Hon. Mrs Havering's application for a housekeeper, and had sent her various applicants for the post. When she sent them the engagement fee, she omitted to mention which woman she had selected.

Somewhat crestfallen, I returned to London. I found Poirot established in an armchair by the fire in a garish, silk dressing-gown. He greeted me with much affection.

'*Mon ami* Hastings! But how glad I am to see you. Veritably I have for you a great affection! And you have enjoyed yourself? You have run to and fro with the good Japp? You have interrogated and investigated to your heart's content?'

'Poirot,' I cried, 'the thing's a dark mystery! It will never be solved.'

'It is true that we are not likely to cover ourselves with glory over it.'

'No, indeed. It's a hard nut to crack.'

'Oh, as far as that goes, I am very good at cracking the nuts! A veritable squirrel! It is not that which embarrasses me. I know well enough who killed Mr Harrington Pace.'

'You know? How did you find out?'

'Your illuminating answers to my wires supplied me with the truth. See here, Hastings, let us examine the facts methodically and in order. Mr Harrington Pace is a man with a considerable fortune which at his death will doubtless pass to his nephew. Point No 1. His nephew is known to be desperately hard up. Point No 2. His nephew is also known to be – shall we say a man of rather loose moral fibre? Point No 3.'

'But Roger Havering is proved to have journeyed straight up to London.'

'*Précisément* – and therefore, as Mr Havering left Elmer's Dale at 6.15, and since Mr Pace cannot have been killed before he left, or the doctor would have spotted the time of the crime as being given wrongly when he examined the body, we conclude quite rightly, that Mr Havering did *not* shoot his uncle. But there is a Mrs Havering, Hastings.'

'Impossible! The housekeeper was with her when the shot was fired.'

'Ah, yes, the housekeeper. But she has disappeared.'

'She will be found.'

'I think not. There is something peculiarly elusive about that housekeeper, don't you think so, Hastings? It struck me at once.'

'She played her part, I suppose, and then got out in the nick of time.'

'And what was her part?'

'Well, presumably to admit her confederate, the black-bearded man.'

'Oh, no, that was not her part! Her part was what you have just mentioned, to provide an alibi for Mrs Havering at the moment the shot was fired. And no one will ever find her, *mon ami*, because she does not exist! "There's no such person," as your so great Shakespeare says.'

'It was Dickens,' I murmured, unable to suppress a smile. 'But what do you mean, Poirot?'

'I mean that Zoe Havering was an actress before her marriage, that you and Japp only saw the housekeeper in a dark hall, a dim middle-aged figure in black with a faint subdued voice, and finally that neither you nor Japp, nor the local police whom the housekeeper fetched, ever saw Mrs Middleton and her mistress at one and the same time. It was child's play for that clever and daring woman. On the pretext of summoning her mistress, she runs upstairs, slips on a bright jumper and a hat with black curls attached which she jams down over the grey transformation. A few deft touches, and the make-up is removed, a slight dusting of rouge, and the brilliant Zoe Havering comes down with her clear ringing voice. Nobody looks particularly at the housekeeper. Why should they? There is nothing to connect her with the crime. She, too, has an alibi.'

'But the revolver that was found at Ealing? Mrs Havering could not have placed it there?'

'No, that was Roger Havering's job – but it was a mistake on their part. It put me on the right track. A man who has committed murder with a revolver which he found on the spot would fling it away at once, he would not carry it up to London with him. No, the motive was clear, the criminals wished to focus the interest of the police on a spot far removed from Derbyshire, they were anxious to get the police away as soon as possible from the vicinity of Hunter's Lodge. Of course the revolver found at Ealing was not the one with which Mr Pace was shot. Roger Havering discharged one shot from it, brought it up to London, went straight to his club to establish his alibi, then went quickly out to Ealing by the District, a matter of about twenty minutes only, placed the parcel where it was found and so back to town. That charming creature, his wife, quietly shoots Mr Pace after dinner – you remember he was shot from behind? Another significant point, that! – reloads the revolver and puts it back in its place, and then starts off with her desperate little comedy.'

'It's incredible,' I muttered, fascinated, 'and yet –'

'And yet it is true. *Bien sur*, my friend, it is true. But to bring that precious pair to justice, that is another matter. Well, Japp must do what he can – I have written him fully – but I very much fear, Hastings, that we shall be obliged to leave them to Fate, or *le bon Dieu*, whichever you prefer.'

'The wicked flourish like a green bay tree,' I reminded him.

'But at a price, Hastings, always at a price, *croyez-moi*!'

Poirot's forebodings were confirmed, Japp, though convinced of the truth of his theory, was unable to get together the necessary evidence to ensure a conviction.

Mr Pace's huge fortune passed into the hands of his murderers. Nevertheless, Nemesis did overtake them, and when I read in the paper that the Hon. Roger and Mrs Havering were amongst those killed in the crashing of the Air Mail to Paris I knew that Justice was satisfied.

Part 5

The Million Dollar Bond Robbery

'What a number of bond robberies there have been lately!' I observed one morning, laying aside the newspaper. 'Poirot, let us forsake the science of detection, and take to crime instead!'

'You are on the – how do you say it? – get-rich-quick tack, eh, *mon ami*?'

'Well, look at this last *coup*, the million dollars' worth of Liberty Bonds which the London and Scottish Bank were sending to New York, and which disappeared in such a remarkable manner on board the *Olympia*.'

'If it were not for *mal de mer*, and the difficulty of practising the so excellent method of Laverguier for a longer time than the few hours of crossing the Channel, I should delight to voyage myself on one of these big liners,' murmured Poirot dreamily.

'Yes, indeed,' I said enthusiastically. 'Some of them

must be perfect palaces; the swimming-baths, the lounges, the restaurant, the palm courts – really, it must be hard to believe that one is on the sea.'

'Me, I always know when I am on the sea,' said Poirot sadly. 'And all those bagatelles that you enumerate, they say nothing to me; but, my friend, consider for a moment the geniuses that travel as it were incognito! On board these floating palaces, as you so justly call them, one would meet the élite, the *haute noblesse* of the criminal world!'

I laughed.

'So that's the way your enthusiasm runs! You would have liked to cross swords with the man who sneaked the Liberty Bonds?'

The landlady interrupted us.

'A young lady as wants to see you, Mr Poirot. Here's her card.'

The card bore the inscription: Miss Esmée Farquhar, and Poirot, after diving under the table to retrieve a stray crumb, and putting it carefully in the waste-paper basket, nodded to the landlady to admit her.

In another minute one of the most charming girls I have ever seen was ushered into the room. She was perhaps about five-and-twenty, with big brown eyes and a perfect figure. She was well-dressed and perfectly composed in manner.

'Sit down, I beg of you, mademoiselle. This is my

friend, Captain Hastings, who aids me in my little problems.'

'I am afraid it is a big problem I have brought you today, Monsieur Poirot,' said the girl, giving me a pleasant bow as she seated herself. 'I dare say you have read about it in the papers. I am referring to the theft of Liberty Bonds on the *Olympia*.' Some astonishment must have shown itself on Poirot's face, for she continued quickly: 'You are doubtless asking yourself what have I to do with a grave institution like the London and Scottish Bank. In one sense nothing, in another sense everything. You see, Monsieur Poirot, I am engaged to Mr Philip Ridgeway.'

'Aha! and Mr Philip Ridgeway –'

'Was in charge of the bonds when they were stolen. Of course no actual blame can attach to him, it was not his fault in any way. Nevertheless, he is half distraught over the matter, and his uncle, I know, insists that he must carelessly have mentioned having them in his possession. It is a terrible setback to his career.'

'Who is his uncle?'

'Mr Vavasour, joint general manager of the London and Scottish Bank.'

'Suppose, Miss Farquhar, that you recount to me the whole story?'

'Very well. As you know, the Bank wished to extend their credits in America, and for this purpose decided to send over a million dollars in Liberty Bonds. Mr Vavasour selected his nephew, who had occupied a position of trust in the Bank for many years and who was conversant with all the details of the Bank's dealings in New York, to make the trip. The *Olympia* sailed from Liverpool on the 23rd, and the bonds were handed over to Philip on the morning of that day by Mr Vavasour and Mr Shaw, the two joint general managers of the London and Scottish Bank. They were counted, enclosed in a package, and sealed in his presence, and he then locked the package at once in his portmanteau.'

'A portmanteau with an ordinary lock?'

'No, Mr Shaw insisted on a special lock being fitted to it by Hubbs. Philip, as I say, placed the package at the bottom of the trunk. It was stolen just a few hours before reaching New York. A rigorous search of the whole ship was made, but without result. The bonds seemed literally to have vanished into thin air.'

Poirot made a grimace.

'But they did not vanish absolutely, since I gather that they were sold in small parcels within half an hour of the docking of the *Olympia*! Well, undoubtedly the next thing is for me to see Mr Ridgeway.'

'I was about to suggest that you should lunch with me at the "Cheshire Cheese". Philip will be there. He is meeting me, but does not yet know that I have been consulting you on his behalf.'

We agreed to this suggestion readily enough, and drove there in a taxi.

Mr Philip Ridgeway was there before us, and looked somewhat surprised to see his fiancée arriving with two complete strangers. He was a nice-looking young fellow, tall and spruce, with a touch of greying hair at the temples, though he could not have been much over thirty.

Miss Farquhar went up to him and laid her hand on his arm.

'You must forgive me acting without consulting you, Philip,' she said. 'Let me introduce you to Monsieur Hercule Poirot, of whom you must often have heard, and his friend, Captain Hastings.'

Ridgeway looked very astonished.

'Of course I have heard of you, Monsieur Poirot,' he said, as he shook hands. 'But I had no idea that Esmée was thinking of consulting you about my – our trouble.'

'I was afraid you would not let me do it, Philip,' said Miss Farquhar meekly.

'So you took care to be on the safe side,' he observed, with a smile. 'I hope Monsieur Poirot will be able to throw some light on this extraordinary puzzle, for I confess frankly that I am nearly out of my mind with worry and anxiety about it.'

Indeed, his face looked drawn and haggard and showed only too clearly the strain under which he was labouring.

'Well, well,' said Poirot. 'Let us lunch, and over lunch we will put our heads together and see what can be done. I want to hear Mr Ridgeway's story from his own lips.'

Whilst we discussed the excellent steak and kidney pudding of the establishment, Philip Ridgeway narrated the circumstances leading to the disappearance of the bonds. His story agreed with that of Miss Farquhar in every particular. When he had finished, Poirot took up the thread with a question.

'What exactly led you to discover that the bonds had been stolen, Mr Ridgeway?'

He laughed rather bitterly.

'The thing stared me in the face, Monsieur Poirot. I couldn't have missed it. My cabin trunk was half out from under the bunk and all scratched and cut about where they'd tried to force the lock.'

'But I understood that it had been opened with a key?'

'That's so. They tried to force it, but couldn't. And in the end, they must have got it unlocked somehow or other.'

'Curious,' said Poirot, his eyes beginning to flicker with the green light I knew so well. 'Very curious! They waste much, much time trying to prise it open, and then – *sapristi*! they find they have the key all the time – for each of Hubbs's locks are unique.'

'That's just why they couldn't have had the key. It never left me day or night.'

'You are sure of that?'

'I can swear to it, and besides, if they had had the key or a duplicate, why should they waste time trying to force an obviously unforceable lock?'

'Ah! there is exactly the question we are asking ourselves! I venture to prophesy that the solution, if we ever find it, will hinge on that curious fact. I beg of you not to assault me if I ask you one more question: *Are you perfectly certain that you did not leave the trunk unlocked*?'

Philip Ridgeway merely looked at him, and Poirot gesticulated apologetically.

'Ah, but these things can happen, I assure you! Very well, the bonds were stolen from the trunk. What did the thief do with them? How did he manage to get ashore with them?'

'Ah!' cried Ridgeway. 'That's just it. How? Word was passed to the Customs authorities, and every soul that left the ship was gone over with a toothcomb!'

'And the bonds, I gather, made a bulky package?'

'Certainly they did. They could hardly have been hidden on board – and anyway we know they weren't, because they were offered for sale within half an hour of the *Olympia's* arrival, long before I got the cables going and the numbers sent out. One broker swears he bought some of them even before the *Olympia* got in. But you can't send bonds by wireless.'

'Not by wireless, but did any tug come alongside?'

'Only the official ones, and that was after the alarm was given when everyone was on the look-out. I was watching out myself for their being passed over to someone that way. My God, Monsieur Poirot, this thing will drive me mad! People are beginning to say I stole them myself.'

'But you also were searched on landing, weren't you?' asked Poirot gently.

'Yes.'

The young man stared at him in a puzzled manner.

'You do not catch my meaning, I see,' said Poirot, smiling enigmatically. 'Now I should like to make a few inquiries at the Bank.'

Ridgeway produced a card and scribbled a few words on it.

'Send this in and my uncle will see you at once.'

Poirot thanked him, bade farewell to Miss Farquhar, and together we started out for Threadneedle Street and the head office of the London and Scottish Bank. On production of Ridgeway's card, we were led through the labyrinth of counters and desks, skirting paying-in clerks and paying-out clerks and up to a small office on the first floor where the joint general managers received us. They were two grave gentlemen, who had grown grey in the service of the Bank. Mr Vavasour had a short white beard, Mr Shaw was clean shaven.

'I understand you are strictly a private inquiry agent?' said Mr Vavasour. 'Quite so, quite so. We have, of course, placed ourselves in the hands of Scotland Yard. Inspector McNeil has charge of the case. A very able officer, I believe.'

'I am sure of it,' said Poirot politely. 'You will permit a few questions, on your nephew's behalf? About this lock, who ordered it from Hubbs's?'

'I ordered it myself,' said Mr Shaw. 'I would not trust to any clerk in the matter. As to the keys, Mr Ridgeway had one, and the other two are held by my colleague and myself.'

'And no clerk has had access to them?'

Mr Shaw turned inquiringly to Mr Vavasour.

'I think I am correct in saying that they have remained in the safe where we placed them on the 23rd,' said Mr Vavasour. 'My colleague was unfortunately taken ill a fortnight ago – in fact on the very day that Philip left us. He has only just recovered.'

'Severe bronchitis is no joke to a man of my age,' said Mr Shaw ruefully. 'But I'm afraid Mr Vavasour has suffered from the hard work entailed by my absence, especially with this unexpected worry coming on top of everything.'

Poirot asked a few more questions. I judged that he was endeavouring to gauge the exact amount of intimacy between uncle and nephew. Mr Vavasour's answers were brief and punctilious. His nephew was a trusted official of the Bank, and had no debts or money difficulties that he knew of. He had been entrusted with similar missions in the past. Finally we were politely bowed out.

'I am disappointed,' said Poirot, as we emerged into the street.

'You hoped to discover more? They are such stodgy old men.'

'It is not their stodginess which disappoints me, *mon ami*. I do not expect to find in a Bank manager, a "keen financier with an eagle glance", as your favourite works of fiction put it. No, I am disappointed in the case – it is too easy!'

'*Easy?*'

'Yes, do you not find it almost childishly simple?'

'You know who stole the bonds?'

'I do.'

'But then – we must – why –'

'Do not confuse and fluster yourself, Hastings. We are not going to do anything at present.'

'But why? What are you waiting for?'

'For the *Olympia*. She is due on her return trip from New York on Tuesday.'

'But if you know who stole the bonds, why wait? He may escape.'

'To a South Sea island where there is no extradition? No, *mon ami*, he would find life very uncongenial there. As to why I wait – *eh bien*, to the intelligence of Hercule Poirot the case is perfectly clear, but for the benefit of others, not so greatly gifted by the good God – the Inspector, McNeil, for instance – it would be as well to make a few inquiries to establish the facts. One must have consideration for those less gifted than oneself.'

'Good Lord, Poirot! Do you know, I'd give a considerable sum of money to see you make a thorough ass of yourself – just for once. You're so confoundedly conceited!'

'Do not enrage yourself, Hastings. In verity, I observe that there are times when you almost detest me! Alas, I suffer the penalties of greatness!'

The little man puffed out his chest, and sighed so comically that I was forced to laugh.

Tuesday saw us speeding to Liverpool in a first-class carriage of the L and NWR. Poirot had obstinately refused to enlighten me as to his suspicions – or certainties. He contented himself with expressing surprise that I, too, was not equally *au fait* with the situation. I disdained to argue, and entrenched my curiosity behind a rampart of pretended indifference.

Once arrived at the quay alongside which lay the big transatlantic liner, Poirot became brisk and alert. Our proceedings consisted in interviewing four successive stewards and inquiring after a friend of Poirot's who had crossed to New York on the 23rd.

'An elderly gentleman, wearing glasses. A great invalid, hardly moved out of his cabin.'

The description appeared to tally with one Mr Ventnor who had occupied the cabin C24 which was next to that of Philip Ridgeway. Although unable to see how Poirot had deduced Mr Ventnor's existence and personal appearance, I was keenly excited.

'Tell me,' I cried, 'was this gentleman one of the first to land when you got to New York?'

The steward shook his head.

'No, indeed, sir, he was one of the last off the boat.'

I retired crestfallen, and observed Poirot grinning at me. He thanked the steward, a note changed hands, and we took our departure.

'It's all very well,' I remarked heatedly, 'but that last answer must have damned your precious theory, grin as you please!'

'As usual, you see nothing, Hastings. That last answer is, on the contrary, the coping-stone of my theory.'

I flung up my hands in despair.

'I give it up.'

II

When we were in the train, speeding towards London, Poirot wrote busily for a few minutes, sealing up the result in an envelope.

'This is for the good Inspector McNeil. We will leave it at Scotland Yard in passing, and then to the Rendezvous Restaurant, where I have asked Miss Esmée Farquhar to do us the honour of dining with us.'

'What about Ridgeway?'

'What about him?' asked Poirot with a twinkle.

'Why, you surely don't think – you can't –'

'The habit of incoherence is growing upon you, Hastings. As a matter of fact I *did* think. If Ridgeway had been the thief – which was perfectly possible – the case would have been charming; a piece of neat methodical work.'

'But not so charming for Miss Farquhar.'

'Possibly you are right. Therefore all is for the best. Now, Hastings, let us review the case. I can see that you are dying to do so. The sealed package is removed from the trunk and vanishes, as Miss Farquhar puts it, into thin air. We will dismiss the thin air theory, which

Agatha Christie

is not practicable at the present stage of science, and consider what is likely to have become of it. Everyone asserts the incredulity of its being smuggled ashore –'

'Yes, but we know –'

'*You* may know, Hastings, I do not. I take the view that, since it seemed incredible, it *was* incredible. Two possibilities remain: it was hidden on board – also rather difficult – or it was thrown overboard.'

'With a cork on it, do you mean?'

'Without a cork.'

I stared.

'But if the bonds were thrown overboard, they couldn't have been sold in New York.'

'I admire your logical mind, Hastings. The bonds were sold in New York, therefore they were not thrown overboard. You see where that leads us?'

'Where we were when we started.'

'*Jamais de la vie*! If the package was thrown overboard and the bonds were sold in New York, the package could not have contained the bonds. Is there any evidence that the package *did* contain the bonds? Remember, Mr Ridgeway never opened it from the time it was placed in his hands in London.'

'Yes, but then –'

Poirot waved an impatient hand.

'Permit me to continue. The last moment that the bonds are seen as bonds is in the office of the London and Scottish Bank on the morning of the 23rd. They reappear in New York half an hour after the *Olympia* gets in, and according to one man, whom nobody listens to, actually *before* she gets in. Supposing then, that they have never been on the Olympia at all? Is there any other way they could get to New York? Yes. The *Gigantic* leaves Southampton on the same day as the *Olympia*, and she holds the record for the Atlantic. Mailed by the *Gigantic*, the bonds would be in New York the day before the *Olympia* arrived. All is clear, the case begins to explain itself. The sealed packet is only a dummy, and the moment of its substitution must be in the office in the bank. It would be an easy matter for any of the three men present to have prepared a duplicate package which could be substituted for the genuine one. *Très bien*, the bonds are mailed to a confederate in New York, with instructions to sell as soon as the *Olympia* is in, but someone must travel on the *Olympia* to engineer the supposed moment of robbery.'

'But why?'

'Because if Ridgeway merely opens the packet and finds it a dummy, suspicion flies at once to London. No, the man on board in the cabin next door does his work, pretends to force the lock in an obvious manner so as to draw immediate attention to the theft, really unlocks the trunk with a duplicate key, throws the package overboard and waits until the last to leave the boat. Naturally he wears glasses to conceal his eyes, and is an invalid since he does not want to run the risk of meeting Ridgeway. He steps ashore in New York and returns by the first boat available.'

'But who – which was he?'

'The man who had a duplicate key, the man who ordered the lock, the man who has *not* been severely ill with bronchitis at his home in the country – *enfin*, the "stodgy" old man, Mr Shaw! There are criminals in high places sometimes, my friend. Ah, here we are, Mademoiselle, I have succeeded! You permit?'

And, beaming, Poirot kissed the astonished girl lightly on either cheek!

Part 6

The Adventure of the Egyptian Tomb

I have always considered that one of the most thrilling and dramatic of the many adventures I have shared with Poirot was that of our investigation into the strange series of deaths which followed upon the discovery and opening of the Tomb of King Men-her-Ra.

Hard upon the discovery of the Tomb of Tutankh-Amen by Lord Carnarvon, Sir John Willard and Mr Bleibner of New York, pursuing their excavations not far from Cairo, in the vicinity of the Pyramids of Gizeh, came unexpectedly on a series of funeral chambers. The greatest interest was aroused by their discovery. The Tomb appeared to be that of King Men-her-Ra, one of those shadowy kings of the Eighth Dynasty, when the Old Kingdom was falling to decay. Little was known about this period, and the discoveries were fully reported in the newspapers.

Agatha Christie

An event soon occurred which took a profound hold on the public mind. Sir John Willard died quite suddenly of heart failure.

The more sensational newspapers immediately took the opportunity of reviving all the old superstitious stories connected with the ill luck of certain Egyptian treasures. The unlucky Mummy at the British Museum, that hoary old chestnut, was dragged out with fresh zest, was quietly denied by the Museum, but nevertheless enjoyed all its usual vogue.

A fortnight later Mr Bleibner died of acute blood poisoning, and a few days afterwards a nephew of his shot himself in New York. The 'Curse of Men-her-Ra' was the talk of the day, and the magic power of dead-and-gone Egypt was exalted to a fetish point.

It was then that Poirot received a brief note from Lady Willard, widow of the dead archaeologist, asking him to go and see her at her house in Kensington Square. I accompanied him.

Lady Willard was a tall, thin woman, dressed in deep mourning. Her haggard face bore eloquent testimony to her recent grief.

'It is kind of you to have come so promptly, Monsieur Poirot.'

'I am at your service, Lady Willard. You wished to consult me?'

'You are, I am aware, a detective, but it is not only

as a detective that I wish to consult you. You are a man of original views, I know, you have imagination, experience of the world; tell me, Monsieur Poirot, what are your views on the supernatural?'

Poirot hesitated for a moment before he replied. He seemed to be considering. Finally he said:

'Let us not misunderstand each other, Lady Willard. It is not a general question that you are asking me there. It has a personal application, has it not? You are referring obliquely to the death of your late husband?'

'That is so,' she admitted.

'You want me to investigate the circumstances of his death?'

'I want you to ascertain for me exactly how much is newspaper chatter, and how much may be said to be founded on fact? Three deaths, Monsieur Poirot – each one explicable taken by itself, but taken together surely an almost unbelievable coincidence, and all within a month of the opening of the tomb! It may be mere superstition, it may be some potent curse from the past that operates in ways undreamed of by modern science. The fact remains – three deaths! And I am afraid, Monsieur Poirot, horribly afraid. It may not yet be the end.'

'For whom do you fear?'

'For my son. When the news of my husband's death came I was ill. My son, who has just come down from

Oxford, went out there. He brought the – the body home, but now he has gone out again, in spite of my prayers and entreaties. He is so fascinated by the work that he intends to take his father's place and carry on the system of excavations. You may think me a foolish, credulous woman, but, Monsieur Poirot, I am afraid. Supposing that the spirit of the dead King is not yet appeased? Perhaps to you I seem to be talking nonsense –'

'No, indeed, Lady Willard,' said Poirot quickly. 'I, too, believe in the force of superstition, one of the greatest forces the world has ever known.'

I looked at him in surprise. I should never have credited Poirot with being superstitious. But the little man was obviously in earnest.

'What you really demand is that I shall protect your son? I will do my utmost to keep him from harm.'

'Yes, in the ordinary way, but against an occult influence?'

'In volumes of the Middle Ages, Lady Willard, you will find many ways of counteracting black magic. Perhaps they knew more than we moderns with all our boasted science. Now let us come to facts, that I may have guidance. Your husband had always been a devoted Egyptologist, hadn't he?'

'Yes, from his youth upwards. He was one of the greatest living authorities upon the subject.'

'But Mr Bleibner, I understand, was more or less of an amateur?'

'Oh, quite. He was a very wealthy man who dabbled freely in any subject that happened to take his fancy. My husband managed to interest him in Egyptology, and it was his money that was so useful in financing the expedition.'

'And the nephew? What do you know of his tastes? Was he with the party at all?'

'I do not think so. In fact I never knew of his existence till I read of his death in the paper. I do not think he and Mr Bleibner can have been at all intimate. He never spoke of having any relations.'

'Who are the other members of the party?'

'Well, there's Dr Tosswill, a minor official connected with the British Museum; Mr Schneider of the Metropolitan Museum in New York; a young American secretary; Dr Ames, who accompanies the expedition in his professional capacity; and Hassan, my husband's devoted native servant.'

'Do you remember the name of the American secretary?'

'Harper, I think, but I cannot be sure. He had not been with Mr Bleibner very long, I know. He was a very pleasant young fellow.'

'Thank you, Lady Willard.'

'If there is anything else –'

'For the moment, nothing. Leave it now in my hands, and be assured that I will do all that is humanly possible to protect your son.'

They were not exactly reassuring words, and I observed Lady Willard wince as he uttered them. Yet, at the same time, the fact that he had not pooh-poohed her fears seemed in itself to be a relief to her.

For my part I had never before suspected that Poirot had so deep a vein of superstition in his nature. I tackled him on the subject as we went homewards. His manner was grave and earnest.

'But yes, Hastings. I believe in these things. You must not underrate the force of superstition.'

'What are we going to do about it?'

'*Toujours pratique*, the good Hastings! *Eh bien*, to begin with we are going to cable to New York for fuller details of young Mr Bleibner's death.'

He duly sent off his cable. The reply was full and precise. Young Rupert Bleibner had been in low water for several years. He had been a beachcomber and a remittance man in several South Sea islands, but had returned to New York two years ago, where he had rapidly sunk lower and lower. The most significant thing, to my mind, was that he had recently managed to borrow enough money to take him to Egypt. 'I've a good friend there I can borrow from,' he had declared. Here, however, his plans had gone awry. He had returned to New York cursing his skinflint of an uncle who cared more for the bones of dead and gone kings than his own flesh and blood. It was during his sojourn in Egypt that the death of Sir John Willard had occurred. Rupert had plunged once more into his life of dissipation in New York, and then, without warning, he had committed suicide, leaving behind him a letter which contained some curious phrases. It seemed written in a sudden fit of remorse. He referred to himself as a leper and an outcast, and the letter ended by declaring that such as he were better dead.

A shadowy theory leapt into my brain. I had never really believed in the vengeance of a long dead Egyptian king. I saw here a more modern crime. Supposing this young man had decided to do away with his uncle – preferably by poison. By mistake, Sir John Willard receives the fatal dose. The young man returns to New York, haunted by his crime. The news of his uncle's death reaches him. He realizes how unnecessary his crime has been, and stricken with remorse takes his own life.

I outlined my solution to Poirot. He was interested.

'It is ingenious what you have thought of there – decidedly it is ingenious. It may even be true. But you leave out of count the fatal influence of the Tomb.'

I shrugged my shoulders.

'You still think that has something to do with it?'

Agatha Christie

'So much so, *mon ami*, that we start for Egypt tomorrow.'

'What?' I cried, astonished.

'I have said it.' An expression of conscious heroism spread over Poirot's face. Then he groaned. 'But oh,' he lamented, 'the sea! The hateful sea!'

II

It was a week later. Beneath our feet was the golden sand of the desert. The hot sun poured down overhead. Poirot, the picture of misery, wilted by my side. The little man was not a good traveller. Our four days' voyage from Marseilles had been one long agony to him. He had landed at Alexandria the wraith of his former self, even his usual neatness had deserted him. We had arrived in Cairo and had driven out at once to the Mena House Hotel, right in the shadow of the Pyramids.

The charm of Egypt had laid hold of me. Not so Poirot. Dressed precisely the same as in London, he carried a small clothes-brush in his pocket and waged an unceasing war on the dust which accumulated on his dark apparel.

'And my boots,' he wailed. 'Regard them, Hastings. My boots, of the neat patent leather, usually so smart and shining. See, the sand is inside them, which is painful, and outside them, which outrages the eyesight. Also the heat, it causes my moustaches to become limp – but limp!'

'Look at the Sphinx,' I urged. 'Even I can feel the mystery and the charm it exhales.'

Poirot looked at it discontentedly.

'It has not the air happy,' he declared. 'How could it, half-buried in sand in that untidy fashion. Ah, this cursed sand!'

'Come, now, there's a lot of sand in Belgium,' I reminded him, mindful of a holiday spent at Knocke-sur-mer in the midst of '*Les dunes impeccables*' as the guide-book had phrased it.

'Not in Brussels,' declared Poirot. He gazed at the Pyramids thoughtfully. 'It is true that they, at least, are of a shape solid and geometrical, but their surface is of an unevenness most unpleasing. And the palm-trees I like them not. Not even do they plant them in rows!'

I cut short his lamentations, by suggesting that we should start for the camp. We were to ride there on camels, and the beasts were patiently kneeling, waiting for us to mount, in charge of several picturesque boys headed by a voluble dragoman.

I pass over the spectacle of Poirot on a camel. He started by groans and lamentations and ended by shrieks, gesticulations and invocations to the Virgin Mary and every Saint in the calendar. In the end, he

Agatha Christie

descended ignominiously and finished the journey on a diminutive donkey. I must admit that a trotting camel is no joke for the amateur. I was stiff for several days.

At last we neared the scene of the excavations. A sunburnt man with a grey beard, in white clothes and wearing a helmet, came to meet us.

'Monsieur Poirot and Captain Hastings? We received your cable. I'm sorry that there was no one to meet you in Cairo. An unforeseen event occurred which completely disorganized our plans.'

Poirot paled. His hand, which had stolen to his clothes-brush, stayed its course.

'Not another death?' he breathed.

'Yes.'

'Sir Guy Willard?' I cried.

'No, Captain Hastings. My American colleague, Mr Schneider.'

'And the cause?' demanded Poirot.

'Tetanus.'

I blanched. All around me I seemed to feel an atmosphere of evil, subtle and menacing. A horrible thought flashed across me. Supposing I were next?

'*Mon Dieu*,' said Poirot, in a very low voice, 'I do not understand this. It is horrible. Tell me, monsieur, there is no doubt that it was tetanus?'

'I believe not. But Dr Ames will tell you more than I can do.'

'Ah, of course, you are not the doctor.'

'My name is Tosswill.'

This, then, was the British expert described by Lady Willard as being a minor official at the British Museum. There was something at once grave and steadfast about him that took my fancy.

'If you will come with me,' continued Dr Tosswill. 'I will take you to Sir Guy Willard. He was most anxious to be informed as soon as you should arrive.'

We were taken across the camp to a large tent. Dr Tosswill lifted up the flap and we entered. Three men were sitting inside.

'Monsieur Poirot and Captain Hastings have arrived, Sir Guy,' said Tosswill.

The youngest of the three men jumped up and came forward to greet us. There was a certain impulsiveness in his manner which reminded me of his mother. He was not nearly so sunburnt as the others, and that fact, coupled with a certain haggardness round the eyes, made him look older than his twenty-two years. He was clearly endeavouring to bear up under a severe mental strain.

He introduced his two companions, Dr Ames, a capable-looking man of thirty-odd, with a touch of greying hair at the temples, and Mr Harper, the secretary, a pleasant lean young man wearing the national insignia of horn-rimmed spectacles.

137

Agatha Christie

After a few minutes' desultory conversation the latter went out, and Dr Tosswill followed him. We were left alone with Sir Guy and Dr Ames.

'Please ask any questions you want to ask, Monsieur Poirot,' said Willard. 'We are utterly dumbfounded at this strange series of disasters, but it isn't – it can't be, anything but coincidence.'

There was a nervousness about his manner which rather belied the words. I saw that Poirot was studying him keenly.

'Your heart is really in this work, Sir Guy?'

'Rather. No matter what happens, or what comes of it, the work is going on. Make up your mind to that.'

Poirot wheeled round on the other.

'What have you to say to that, *monsieur le docteur*?'

'Well,' drawled the doctor, 'I'm not for quitting myself.'

Poirot made one of those expressive grimaces of his.

'Then, *évidemment*, we must find out just how we stand. When did Mr Schneider's death take place?'

'Three days ago.'

'You are sure it was tetanus?'

'Dead sure.'

'It couldn't have been a case of strychnine poisoning, for instance?'

'No, Monsieur Poirot, I see what you are getting at. But it was a clear case of tetanus.'

'Did you not inject anti-serum?'

'Certainly we did,' said the doctor dryly. 'Every conceivable thing that could be done was tried.'

'Had you the anti-serum with you?'

'No. We procured it from Cairo.'

'Have there been any other cases of tetanus in the camp?'

'No, not one.'

'Are you certain that the death of Mr Bleibner was not due to tetanus?'

'Absolutely plumb certain. He had a scratch upon his thumb which became poisoned, and septicaemia set in. It sounds pretty much the same to a layman, I dare say, but the two things are entirely different.'

'Then we have four deaths – all totally dissimilar, one heart failure, one blood poisoning, one suicide and one tetanus.'

'Exactly, Monsieur Poirot.'

'Are you certain that there is nothing which might link the four together?'

'I don't quite understand you?'

'I will put it plainly. Was any act committed by those four men which might seem to denote disrespect to the spirit of Men-her-Ra?'

The doctor gazed at Poirot in astonishment.

Agatha Christie

'You're talking through your hat, Monsieur Poirot. Surely you've not been guyed into believing all that fool talk?'

'Absolute nonsense,' muttered Willard angrily.

Poirot remained placidly immovable, blinking a little out of his green cat's eyes.

'So you do not believe it, *monsieur le docteur*?'

'No, sir, I do not,' declared the doctor emphatically. 'I am a scientific man, and I believe only what science teaches.'

'Was there no science then in Ancient Egypt?' asked Poirot softly. He did not wait for a reply, and indeed Dr Ames seemed rather at a loss for the moment. 'No, no, do not answer me, but tell me this. What do the native workmen think?'

'I guess,' said Dr Ames, 'that, where white folk lose their heads, natives aren't going to be far behind. I'll admit that they're getting what you might call scared – but they've no cause to be.'

'I wonder,' said Poirot non-committally.

Sir Guy leant forward.

'Surely,' he cried incredulously, 'you cannot believe in – oh, but the thing's absurd! You can know nothing of Ancient Egypt if you think that.'

For answer Poirot produced a little book from his pocket – an ancient tattered volume. As he held it out I saw its title, *The Magic of the Egyptians and Chaldeans*.

140

Then, wheeling round, he strode out of the tent. The doctor stared at me.

'What is his little idea?'

The phrase, so familiar on Poirot's lips, made me smile as it came from another.

'I don't know exactly,' I confessed. 'He's got some plan of exorcizing the evil spirits, I believe.'

I went in search of Poirot, and found him talking to the lean-faced young man who had been the late Mr Bleibner's secretary.

'No,' Mr Harper was saying, 'I've only been six months with the expedition. Yes, I knew Mr Bleibner's affairs pretty well.'

'Can you recount to me anything concerning his nephew?'

'He turned up here one day, not a bad-looking fellow. I'd never met him before, but some of the others had – Ames, I think, and Schneider. The old man wasn't at all pleased to see him. They were at it in no time, hammer and tongs. "Not a cent," the old man shouted. "Not one cent now or when I'm dead. I intend to leave my money to the furtherance of my life's work. I've been talking it over with Mr Schneider today." And a bit more of the same. Young Bleibner lit out for Cairo right away.'

'Was he in perfectly good health at the time?'

'The old man?'

'No, the young one.'

'I believe he did mention there was something wrong with him. But it couldn't have been anything serious, or I should have remembered.'

'One thing more, has Mr Bleibner left a will?'

'So far as we know, he has not.'

'Are you remaining with the expedition, Mr Harper?'

'No, sir, I am not. I'm for New York as soon as I can square up things here. You may laugh if you like, but I'm not going to be this blasted Men-her-Ra's next victim. He'll get me if I stop here.'

The young man wiped the perspiration from his brow.

Poirot turned away. Over his shoulder he said with a peculiar smile:

'Remember, he got one of his victims in New York.'

'Oh, hell!' said Mr Harper forcibly.

'That young man is nervous,' said Poirot thoughtfully. 'He is on the edge, but absolutely on the edge.'

I glanced at Poirot curiously, but his enigmatical smile told me nothing. In company with Sir Guy Willard and Dr Tosswill we were taken round the excavations. The principal finds had been removed to Cairo, but some of the tomb furniture was extremely interesting. The enthusiasm of the young baronet was obvious, but I fancied that I detected a shade of nervousness in his manner as though he could not quite escape from the feeling of menace in the air. As we entered the tent which had been assigned to us, for a wash before joining the evening meal, a tall dark figure in white robes stood aside to let us pass with a graceful gesture and a murmured greeting in Arabic. Poirot stopped.

'You are Hassan, the late Sir John Willard's servant?'

'I served my Lord Sir John, now I serve his son.' He took a step nearer to us and lowered his voice. 'You are a wise one, they say, learned in dealing with evil spirits. Let the young master depart from here. There is evil in the air around us.'

And with an abrupt gesture, not waiting for a reply, he strode away.

'Evil in the air,' muttered Poirot. 'Yes, I feel it.'

Our meal was hardly a cheerful one. The floor was left to Dr Tosswill, who discoursed at length upon Egyptian antiquities. Just as we were preparing to retire to rest, Sir Guy caught Poirot by the arm and pointed. A shadowy figure was moving amidst the tents. It was no human one: I recognized distinctly the dog-headed figure I had seen carved on the walls of the tomb.

My blood froze at the sight.

'*Mon Dieu!*' murmured Poirot, crossing himself vigorously. 'Anubis, the jackal-headed, the god of departing souls.'

Agatha Christie

'Someone is hoaxing us,' cried Dr Tosswill, rising indignantly to his feet.

'It went into your tent, Harper,' muttered Sir Guy, his face dreadfully pale.

'No,' said Poirot, shaking his head, 'into that of the Dr Ames.'

The doctor stared at him incredulously; then, repeating Dr Tosswill's words, he cried:

'Someone is hoaxing us. Come, we'll soon catch the fellow.'

He dashed energetically in pursuit of the shadowy apparition. I followed him, but, search as we would, we could find no trace of any living soul having passed that way. We returned, somewhat disturbed in mind, to find Poirot taking energetic measures, in his own way, to ensure his personal safety. He was busily surrounding our tent with various diagrams and inscriptions which he was drawing in the sand. I recognized the five-pointed star or Pentagon many times repeated. As was his wont, Poirot was at the same time delivering an impromptu lecture on witchcraft and magic in general, White magic as opposed to Black, with various references to the Ka and the Book of the Dead thrown in.

It appeared to excite the liveliest contempt in Dr Tosswill, who drew me aside, literally snorting with rage.

'Balderdash, sir,' he exclaimed angrily. 'Pure balder-dash. The man's an imposter. He doesn't know the difference between the superstitions of the Middle Ages and the beliefs of Ancient Egypt. Never have I heard such a hotch-potch of ignorance and cred-ulity.'

I calmed the excited expert, and joined Poirot in the tent. My little friend was beaming cheerfully.

'We can now sleep in peace,' he declared happily. 'And I can do with some sleep. My head, it aches abominably. Ah, for a good *tisane!*'

As though in answer to prayer, the flap of the tent was lifted and Hassan appeared, bearing a steaming cup which he offered to Poirot. It proved to be camomile tea, a beverage of which he is inordinately fond. Having thanked Hassan and refused his offer of another cup for myself, we were left alone once more. I stood at the door of the tent some time after undressing, looking out over the desert.

'A wonderful place,' I said aloud, 'and a wonderful work. I can feel the fascination. This desert life, this probing into the heart of a vanished civilization. Surely, Poirot, you, too, must feel the charm?'

I got no answer, and I turned, a little annoyed. My annoyance was quickly changed to concern. Poirot was lying back across the rude couch, his face horribly convulsed. Beside him was the empty cup. I rushed to his side, then dashed out and across the camp to Dr Ames's tent.

'Dr Ames!' I cried. 'Come at once.'

'What's the matter?' said the doctor, appearing in pyjamas.

'My friend. He's ill. Dying. The camomile tea. Don't let Hassan leave the camp.'

Like a flash the doctor ran to our tent. Poirot was lying as I left him.

'Extraordinary,' cried Ames. 'Looks like a seizure – or – what did you say about something he drank?' He picked up the empty cup.

'Only I did not drink it!' said a placid voice.

We turned in amazement. Poirot was sitting up on the bed. He was smiling.

'No,' he said gently. 'I did not drink it. While my good friend Hastings was apostrophizing the night, I took the opportunity of pouring it, not down my throat, but into a little bottle. That little bottle will go to the analytical chemist. No' – as the doctor made a sudden movement – 'as a sensible man, you will understand that violence will be of no avail. During Hastings' absence to fetch you, I have had time to put the bottle in safe keeping. Ah, quick, Hastings, hold him!'

I misunderstood Poirot's anxiety. Eager to save my friend, I flung myself in front of him. But the doctor's swift movement had another meaning. His hand went to his mouth, a smell of bitter almonds filled the air, and he swayed forward and fell.

'Another victim,' said Poirot gravely, 'but the last. Perhaps it is the best way. He has three deaths on his head.'

'Dr Ames?' I cried, stupefied. 'But I thought you believed in some occult influence?'

'You misunderstood me, Hastings. What I meant was that I believe in the terrific force of superstition. Once get it firmly established that a series of deaths are supernatural, and you might almost stab a man in broad daylight, and it would still be put down to the curse, so strongly is the instinct of the supernatural implanted in the human race. I suspected from the first that a man was taking advantage of that instinct. The idea came to him, I imagine, with the death of Sir John Willard. A fury of superstition arose at once. As far as I could see, nobody could derive any particular profit from Sir John's death. Mr Bleibner was a different case. He was a man of great wealth. The information I received from New York contained several suggestive points. To begin with, young Bleibner was reported to have said he had a good friend in Egypt from whom he could borrow. It was tacitly understood that he meant his uncle, but it seemed to me that in that case he would have said so outright. The words suggest some boon companion of his own. Another thing, he scraped up

147

enough money to take him to Egypt, his uncle refused outright to advance him a penny, yet he was able to pay the return passage to New York. Someone must have lent him the money.'

'All that was very thin,' I objected.

'But there was more. Hastings, there occur often enough words spoken metaphorically which are taken literally. The opposite can happen too. In this case, words which were meant literally were taken metaphorically. Young Bleibner wrote plainly enough: "I am a leper," but nobody realized that he shot himself because he believed that he contracted the dread disease of leprosy.'

'What?' I ejaculated.

'It was the clever invention of a diabolical mind. Young Bleibner was suffering from some minor skin trouble; he had lived in the South Sea Islands, where the disease is common enough. Ames was a former friend of his, and a well-known medical man, he would never dream of doubting his word. When I arrived here, my suspicions were divided between Harper and Dr Ames, but I soon realized that only the doctor could have perpetrated and concealed the crimes, and I learn from Harper that he was previously acquainted with young Bleibner. Doubtless the latter at some time or another had made a will or had insured his life in favour of the doctor. The latter saw his chance of acquiring wealth. It was easy for him to inoculate Mr Bleibner with the deadly germs. Then the nephew, overcome with despair at the dread news his friend had conveyed to him, shot himself. Mr Bleibner, whatever his intentions, had made no will. His fortune would pass to his nephew and from him to the doctor.'

'And Mr Schneider?'

'We cannot be sure. He knew young Bleibner too, remember, and may have suspected something, or, again, the doctor may have thought that a further death motiveless and purposeless would strengthen the coils of superstition. Furthermore, I will tell you an interesting psychological fact, Hastings. A murderer has always a strong desire to repeat his successful crime, the performance of it grows upon him. Hence my fears for young Willard. The figure of Anubis you saw tonight was Hassan dressed up by my orders. I wanted to see if I could frighten the doctor. But it would take more than the supernatural to frighten him. I could see that he was not entirely taken in by my pretences of belief in the occult. The little comedy I played for him did not deceive him. I suspected that he would endeavour to make me the next victim. Ah, but in spite of *la mer maudite*, the heat abominable, and the annoyances of the sand, the little grey cells still functioned!'

Poirot proved to be perfectly right in his premises. Young Bleibner, some years ago, in a fit of drunken merriment, had made a jocular will, leaving 'my cigarette-case you admire so much and everything else of which I die possessed which will be principally debts to my good friend Robert Ames who once saved my life from drowning'.

The case was hushed up as far as possible, and, to this day, people talk of the remarkable series of deaths in connection with the Tomb of Men-her-Ra as a triumphal proof of the vengeance of a bygone king upon the desecrators of his tomb – a belief which, as Poirot pointed out to me, is contrary to all Egyptian belief and thought.

Part 7

The Jewel Robbery at the Grand Metropolitan

'Poirot,' I said, 'a change of air would do you good.'

'You think so, *mon ami*?'

'I am sure of it.'

'Eh – eh?' said my friend, smiling. 'It is all arranged, then?'

'You will come?'

'Where do you propose to take me?'

'Brighton. As a matter of fact, a friend of mine in the City put me on to a very good thing, and – well, I have money to burn, as the saying goes. I think a weekend at the Grand Metropolitan would do us all the good in the world.'

'Thank you, I accept most gratefully. You have the good heart to think of an old man. And the good heart, it is in the end worth all the little grey cells. Yes, yes, I who speak to you am in danger of forgetting that sometimes.'

I did not relish the implication. I fancy that Poirot is sometimes a little inclined to underestimate my mental capacities. But his pleasure was so evident that I put my slight annoyance aside.

'Then, that's all right,' I said hastily.

Saturday evening saw us dining at the Grand Metropolitan in the midst of a gay throng. All the world and his wife seemed to be at Brighton. The dresses were marvellous, and the jewels – worn sometimes with more love of display than good taste – were something magnificent.

'*Hein*, it is a good sight, this!' murmured Poirot. 'This is the home of the Profiteer, is it not so, Hastings?'

'Supposed to be,' I replied. 'But we'll hope they aren't all tarred with the Profiteering brush.'

Poirot gazed round him placidly.

'The sight of so many jewels makes me wish I had turned my brains to crime, instead of to its detection. What a magnificent opportunity for some thief of distinction! Regard, Hastings, that stout woman by the pillar. She is, as you would say, plastered with gems.'

I followed his eyes.

'Why,' I exclaimed, 'it's Mrs Opalsen.'

'You know her?'

'Slightly. Her husband is a rich stockbroker who made a fortune in the recent oil boom.'

After dinner we ran across the Opalsens in the lounge, and I introduced Poirot to them. We chatted for a few minutes, and ended by having our coffee together.

Poirot said a few words in praise of some of the costlier gems displayed on the lady's ample bosom, and she brightened up at once.

'It's a perfect hobby of mine, Mr Poirot. I just *love* jewellery. Ed knows my weakness, and every time things go well he brings me something new. You are interested in precious stones?'

'I have had a good deal to do with them one time and another, madame. My profession has brought me into contact with some of the most famous jewels in the world.'

He went on to narrate, with discreet pseudonyms, the story of the historic jewels of a reigning house, and Mrs Opalsen listened with bated breath.

'There now,' she exclaimed, as he ended. 'If it isn't just like a play! You know, I've got some pearls of my own that have a history attached to them. I believe it's supposed to be one of the finest necklaces in the world – the pearls are so beautifully matched and so perfect in colour. I declare I really must run up and get it!'

'Oh, madame,' protested Poirot, 'you are too amiable. Pray do not derange yourself!'

'Oh, but I'd like to show it to you.'

153

The buxom dame waddled across to the lift briskly enough. Her husband, who had been talking to me, looked at Poirot inquiringly.

'Madame your wife is so amiable as to insist on showing me her pearl necklace,' explained the latter.

'Oh, the pearls!' Opalsen smiled in a satisfied fashion. 'Well, they *are* worth seeing. Cost a pretty penny too! Still, the money's there all right; I could get what I paid for them any day – perhaps more. May have to, too, if things go on as they are now. Money's confoundedly tight in the City. All this infernal EPD.' He rambled on, launching into technicalities where I could not follow him.

He was interrupted by a small page-boy who approached him and murmured something in his ear.

'Eh – what? I'll come at once. Not taken ill, is she? Excuse me, gentlemen.'

He left us abruptly. Poirot leaned back and lit one of his tiny Russian cigarettes. Then, carefully and meticulously, he arranged the empty coffee-cups in a neat row, and beamed happily on the result.

The minutes passed. The Opalsens did not return.

'Curious,' I remarked, at length. 'I wonder when they will come back.'

Poirot watched the ascending spirals of smoke, and then said thoughtfully:

'They will not come back.'

'Why?'

'Because, my friend, something has happened.'

'What sort of thing? How do you know?' I asked curiously.

Poirot smiled.

'A few minutes ago the manager came hurriedly out of his office and ran upstairs. He was much agitated. The liftboy is deep in talk with one of the pages. The lift-bell has rung three times, but he heeds it not. Thirdly, even the waiters are *distrait*; and to make a waiter *distrait* –' Poirot shook his head with an air of finality. 'The affair must indeed be of the first magnitude. Ah, it is as I thought! Here come the police.'

Two men had just entered the hotel – one in uniform, the other in plain clothes. They spoke to a page, and were immediately ushered upstairs. A few minutes later, the same boy descended and came up to where we were sitting.

'Mr Opalsen's compliments, and would you step upstairs?'

Poirot sprang nimbly to his feet. One would have said that he awaited the summons. I followed with no less alacrity.

The Opalsens' apartments were situated on the first floor. After knocking on the door, the page-boy retired, and we answered the summons. 'Come in!' A strange

155

scene met our eyes. The room was Mrs Opalsen's bed-room, and in the centre of it, lying back in an armchair, was the lady herself, weeping violently. She presented an extraordinary spectacle, with the tears making great furrows in the powder with which her complexion was liberally coated. Mr Opalsen was striding up and down angrily. The two police officials stood in the middle of the room, one with a notebook in hand. An hotel chambermaid, looking frightened to death, stood by the fireplace; and on the other side of the room a Frenchwoman, obviously Mrs Opalsen's maid, was weeping and wringing her hands, with an intensity of grief that rivalled that of her mistress.

Into this pandemonium stepped Poirot, neat and smiling. Immediately, with an energy surprising in one of her bulk Mrs Opalsen sprang from her chair towards him.

'There now; Ed may say what he likes, but I believe in luck, I do. It was fated I should meet you the way I did this evening, and I've a feeling that if you can't get my pearls back for me nobody can.'

'Calm yourself, I pray of you, madame.' Poirot patted her hand soothingly. 'Reassure yourself. All will be well. Hercule Poirot will aid you!'

Mr Opalsen turned to the police inspector.

'There will be no objection to my – er – calling in this gentleman, I suppose?'

'None at all, sir,' replied the man civilly, but with complete indifference. 'Perhaps now your lady's feeling better she'll just let us have the facts?'

Mrs Opalsen looked helplessly at Poirot. He led her back to her chair.

'Seat yourself, madame, and recount to us the whole history without agitating yourself.'

Thus abjured, Mrs Opalsen dried her eyes gingerly, and began.

'I came upstairs after dinner to fetch my pearls for Mr Poirot here to see. The chambermaid and Célestine were both in the room as usual –'

'Excuse me, madame, but what do you mean by "as usual"?'

Mr Opalsen explained.

'I make it a rule that no one is to come into this room unless Célestine, the maid, is there also. The chambermaid does the room in the morning while Célestine is present, and comes in after dinner to turn down the beds under the same conditions; otherwise she never enters the room.'

'Well, as I was saying,' continued Mrs Opalsen, 'I came up. I went to the drawer here' – she indicated the bottom right-hand drawer of the knee-hole dressing-table – 'took out my jewel-case and unlocked it. It seemed quite as usual – but the pearls were not there!'

The inspector had been busy with his notebook. When had you last seen them?' he asked.

'They were there when I went down to dinner.'

'You are sure?'

'Quite sure. I was uncertain whether to wear them or not, but in the end I decided on the emeralds, and put them back in the jewel-case.'

'Who locked up the jewel-case?'

'I did. I wear the key on a chain round my neck.' She held it up as she spoke.

The inspector examined it, and shrugged his shoulders.

'The thief must have had a duplicate key. No difficult matter. The lock is quite a simple one. What did you do after you'd locked the jewel-case?'

'I put it back in the bottom drawer where I always keep it.'

'You didn't lock the drawer?'

'No, I never do. My maid remains in the room till I come up, so there's no need.'

The inspector's face grew greyer.

'Am I to understand that the jewels were there when you went down to dinner, and that since then *the maid has not left the room*?'

Suddenly, as though the horror of her own situation for the first time burst upon her, Célestine uttered a piercing shriek, and, flinging herself upon Poirot, poured out a torrent of incoherent French.

The suggestion was infamous! That she should be suspected of robbing Madame! The police were well known to be of a stupidity incredible! But Monsieur, who was a Frenchman –'

'A Belgian,' interjected Poirot, but Célestine paid no attention to the correction.

Monsieur would not stand by and see her falsely accused, while that infamous chambermaid was allowed to go scot-free. She had never liked her – a bold, red-faced thing – a born thief. She had said from the first that she was not honest. And had kept a sharp watch over her too, when she was doing Madame's room! Let those idiots of policemen search her, and if they did not find Madame's pearls on her it would be very surprising!

Although this harangue was uttered in rapid and virulent French, Célestine had interlarded it with a wealth of gesture, and the chambermaid realized at least a part of her meaning. She reddened angrily.

'If that foreign woman's saying I took the pearls, it's a lie!' she declared heatedly. 'I never so much as saw them.'

'Search her!' screamed the other. 'You will find it is as I say.'

'You're a lair – do you hear?' said the chambermaid, advancing upon her. 'Stole 'em yourself, and want to put it on me. Why, I was only in the room about three minutes before the lady came up, and then you were sitting here the whole time, as you always do, like a cat watching a mouse.'

The inspector looked across inquiringly at Célestine. 'Is that true? Didn't you leave the room at all?'

'I did not actually leave her alone,' admitted Célestine reluctantly, 'but I went into my own room through the door here twice – once to fetch a reel of cotton, and once for my scissors. She must have done it then.'

'You wasn't gone a minute,' retorted the chambermaid angrily. 'Just popped out and in again. I'd be glad if the police *would* search me. *I've* nothing to be afraid of.'

At this moment there was a tap at the door. The inspector went to it. His face brightened when he saw who it was.

'Ah!' he said. 'That's rather fortunate. I sent for one of our female searchers, and she's just arrived. Perhaps if you wouldn't mind going into the room next door.'

He looked at the chambermaid, who stepped across the threshold with a toss of her head, the searcher following her closely.

The French girl had sunk sobbing into a chair. Poirot was looking round the room, the main features of which I have made clear by a sketch.

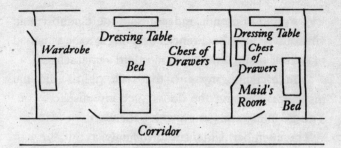

'Where does that door lead?' he inquired, nodding his head towards the one by the window.

'Into the next apartment, I believe,' said the inspector. 'It's bolted, anyway, on this side.'

Poirot walked across to it, tried it, then drew back the bolt and tried it again.

'And on the other side as well,' he remarked. 'Well, that seems to rule out that.'

He walked over to the windows, examining each of them in turn.

'And again – nothing. Not even a balcony outside.'

'Even if there were,' said the inspector impatiently, 'I don't see how that would help us, if the maid never left the room.'

'*Évidemment*,' said Poirot, not disconcerted. 'As Mademoiselle is positive she did not leave the room –'

He was interrupted by the reappearance of the chambermaid and the police searcher.

'Nothing,' said the latter laconically.

161

'I should hope not, indeed,' said the chambermaid virtuously. 'And that French hussy ought to be ashamed of herself taking away an honest girl's character.'

'There, there, my girl; that's all right,' said the inspector, opening the door. 'Nobody suspects you. You go along and get on with your work.'

The chambermaid went unwillingly.

'Going to search *her*?' she demanded, pointing at Célestine.

'Yes, yes!' He shut the door on her and turned the key.

Célestine accompanied the searcher into the small room in her turn. A few minutes later she also returned. Nothing had been found on her.

The inspector's face grew graver.

'I'm afraid I'll have to ask you to come along with me all the same, miss.' He turned to Mrs Opalsen. 'I'm sorry, madam, but all the evidence points that way. If she's not got them on her, they're hidden somewhere about the room.'

Célestine uttered a piercing shriek, and clung to Poirot's arm. The latter bent and whispered something in the girl's ear. She looked up at him doubtfully.

'*Si, si, mon enfant* – I assure you it is better not to resist.' Then he turned to the inspector. 'You permit, monsieur? A little experiment – purely for my own satisfaction.'

162

'Depends on what it is,' replied the police officer noncommittally.

Poirot addressed Célestine once more.

'You have told us that you went into your room to fetch a reel of cotton. Whereabouts was it?'

'On top of the chest of drawers, monsieur.'

'And the scissors?'

'They also.'

'Would it be troubling you too much, mademoiselle, to ask you to repeat those two actions? You were sitting here with your work, you say?'

Célestine sat down, and then, at a sign from Poirot, rose, passed into the adjoining room, took up an object from the chest of drawers, and returned.

Poirot divided his attention between her movements and a large turnip of a watch which he held in the palm of his hand.

'Again, if you please, mademoiselle.'

At the conclusion of the second performance, he made a note in his pocket-book, and returned the watch to his pocket.

'Thank you, mademoiselle. And you, monsieur' – he bowed to the inspector – 'for your courtesy.'

The inspector seemed somewhat entertained by this excessive politeness. Célestine departed in a flood of tears, accompanied by the woman and the plain-clothes official.

Then, with a brief apology to Mrs Opalsen, the inspector set to work to ransack the room. He pulled out drawers, opened cupboards, completely unmade the bed, and tapped the floor. Mr Opalsen looked on sceptically.

'You really think you will find them?'

'Yes, sir. It stands to reason. She hadn't time to take them out of the room. The lady's discovering the robbery so soon upset her plans. No, they're here right enough. One of the two must have hidden them – and it's very unlikely for the chambermaid to have done so.'

'More than unlikely – impossible!' said Poirot quietly.

'Eh?' The inspector stared.

Poirot smiled modestly.

'I will demonstrate. Hastings, my good friend, take my watch in your hand – with care. It is a family heirloom! Just now I timed Mademoiselle's movements – her first absence from the room was of twelve seconds, her second of fifteen. Now observe my actions. Madame will have the kindness to give me the key of the jewel-case. I thank you. My friend Hastings will have the kindness to say "Go!"'

'Go!' I said.

With almost incredible swiftness, Poirot wrenched open the drawer of the dressing-table, extracted the jewel-case, fitted the key in the lock, opened the case, selected a piece of jewellery, shut and locked the case, and returned it to the drawer, which he pushed to again. His movements were like lightning.

'Well, *mon ami*?' he demanded of me breathlessly.

'Forty-six seconds,' I replied.

'You see?' He looked round. 'There would have not been time for the chambermaid even to take the necklace out, far less hide it.'

'Then that settles it on the maid,' said the inspector with satisfaction, and returned to his search. He passed into the maid's bedroom next door.

Poirot was frowning thoughtfully. Suddenly he shot a question at Mr Opalsen.

'This necklace – it was, without doubt, insured?'

Mr Opalsen looked a trifle surprised at the question.

'Yes,' he said hesitatingly, 'that is so.'

'But what does that matter?' broke in Mrs Opalsen tearfully. 'It's my necklace I want. It was unique. No money could be the same.'

'I comprehend, madame,' said Poirot soothingly. 'I comprehend perfectly. To *la femme* sentiment is everything – is it not so? But, monsieur, who has not the so fine susceptibility, will doubtless find some slight consolation in the fact.'

'Of course, of course,' said Mr Opalsen rather uncertainly. 'Still –'

He was interrupted by a shout of triumph from the inspector. He came in dangling something from his fingers.

With a cry, Mrs Opalsen heaved herself up from her chair. She was a changed woman.

'Oh, oh, my necklace!'

She clasped it to her breast with both hands. We crowded round.

'Where was it?' demanded Opalsen.

'Maid's bed. In among the springs of the wire mattress. She must have stolen it and hidden it there before the chambermaid arrived on the scene.'

'You permit, madame?' said Poirot gently. He took the necklace from her and examined it closely; then handed it back with a bow.

'I'm afraid, madame, you'll have to hand it over to us for the time being,' said the inspector. 'We shall want it for the charge. But it shall be returned to you as soon as possible.'

Mr Opalsen frowned.

'Is that necessary?'

'I'm afraid so, sir. Just a formality.'

'Oh, let him take it, Ed!' cired his wife. 'I'd feel safer if he did. I shouldn't sleep a wink thinking someone else might try to get hold of it. That wretched girl! And I would never have believed it of her.'

'There, there, my dear, don't take on so.'

I felt a gentle pressure on my arm. It was Poirot.

'Shall we slip away, my friend? I think our services are no longer needed.'

Once outside, however, he hesitated, and then, much to my surprise, he remarked:

'I should rather like to see the room next door.'

The door was not locked, and we entered. The room, which was a large double one, was unoccupied. Dust lay about rather noticeably, and my sensitive friend gave a characteristic grimace as he ran his finger round a rectangular mark on a table near the window.

'The *service* leaves to be desired,' he observed dryly.

He was staring thoughtfully out of the window, and seemed to have fallen into a brown study.

'Well?' I demanded impatiently. 'What did we come in here for?'

He started.

'*Je vous demande pardon, mon ami.* I wished to see if the door was really bolted on this side also.'

'Well,' I said, glancing at the door which communicated with the room we had just left, 'it *is* bolted.'

Poirot nodded. He still seemed to be thinking.

'And anyway,' I continued, 'what does it matter? The case is over. I wish you'd had more chance of distinguishing yourself. But it was the kind of case that even a stiff-backed idiot like that inspector couldn't go wrong over.'

Poirot shook his head.

'The case is not over, my friend. It will not be over until we find out who stole the pearls.'

'But the maid did!'

'Why do you say that?'

'Why,' I stammered, 'they were found – actually in her mattress.'

'Ta, ta, ta!' said Poirot impatiently. 'Those were not the pearls.'

'What?'

'Imitation, *mon ami*.'

The statement took my breath away. Poirot was smiling placidly.

'The good inspector obviously knows nothing of jewels. But presently there will be a fine hullaba-loo!'

'Come!' I cried, dragging at his arm.

'Where?'

'We must tell the Opalsens at once.'

'I think not.'

'But that poor woman –'

'*Eh bien*; that poor woman, as you call her, will have a much better night believing the jewels to be safe.'

'But the thief may escape with them!'

'As usual, my friend, you speak without reflection. How do you know that the pearls Mrs Opalsen locked up so carefully tonight were not the false ones, and that the real robbery did not take place at a much earlier date?'

'Oh!' I said, bewildered.

'Exactly,' said Poirot, beaming. 'We start again.'

He led the way out of the room, paused a moment as though considering, and then walked down to the end of the corridor, stopping outside the small den where the chambermaids and valets of the respective floors congregated. Our particular chambermaid appeared to be holding a small court there, and to be retailing her late experiences to an appreciative audience. She stopped in the middle of a sentence. Poirot bowed with his usual politeness.

'Excuse that I derange you, but I shall be obliged if you will unlock for me the door of Mr Opalsen's room.'

The woman rose willingly, and we accompanied her down the passage again. Mr Opalsen's room was on the other side of the corridor, its door facing that of his wife's room. The chambermaid unlocked it with her pass-key, and we entered.

As she was about to depart Poirot detained her.

'One moment; have you ever seen among the effects of Mr Opalsen a card like this?'

He held out a plain white card, rather highly glazed and uncommon in appearance. The maid took it and scrutinized it carefully.

'No, sir, I can't say I have. But, anyway, the valet has most to do with the gentlemen's rooms.'

'I see. Thank you.'

Poirot took back the card. The woman departed. Poirot appeared to reflect a little. Then he gave a short, sharp nod of the head.

'Ring the bell, I pray you, Hastings. Three times for the valet.'

I obeyed, devoured with curiosity. Meanwhile Poirot had emptied the waste-paper basket on the floor, and was swiftly going through its contents.

In a few moments the valet answered the bell. To him Poirot put the same question, and handed him the card to examine. But the response was the same. The valet had never seen a card of that particular quality among Mr Opalsen's belongings. Poirot thanked him, and he withdrew, somewhat unwillingly, with an inquisitive glance at the overturned waste-paper basket and the litter on the floor. He could hardly have helped over-hearing Poirot's thoughtful remark as he bundled the torn papers back again:

'And the necklace was heavily insured . . .'

'Poirot,' I cried, 'I see –'

'You see nothing, my friend,' he replied quickly. 'As

usual, nothing at all! It is incredible – but there it is. Let us return to our own apartments.'

We did so in silence. Once there, to my intense surprise, Poirot effected a rapid change of clothing.

'I go to London tonight,' he explained. 'It is imperative.'

'What?'

'Absolutely. The real work, that of the brain (ah, those brave little grey cells), it is done. I go to seek the confirmation. I shall find it! Impossible to deceive Hercule Poirot!'

'You'll come a cropper one of these days,' I observed, rather disgusted by his vanity.

'Do not be enraged, I beg of you, *mon ami*. I count on you to do me a service – of your friendship.'

'Of course,' I said eagerly, rather ashamed of my moroseness. 'What is it?'

'The sleeve of my coat that I have taken off – will you brush it? See you, a little white powder has clung to it. You without doubt observed me run my finger round the drawer of the dressing-table?'

'No, I didn't.'

'You should observe my actions, my friend. Thus I obtained the powder on my finger, and, being a little overexcited, I rubbed it on my sleeve; an action without method which I deplore – false to all my principles.'

'But what was the powder?' I asked, not particularly interested in Poirot's principles.

'Not the poison of the Borgias,' replied Poirot with a twinkle. 'I see your imagination mounting. I should say it was French chalk.'

'French chalk?'

'Yes, cabinet-makers use it to make drawers run smoothly.'

I laughed.

'You old sinner! I thought you were working up to something exciting.'

'Au revoir, my friend. I save myself. I fly!'

The door shut behind him. With a smile, half of derision, half of affection, I picked up the coat and stretched out my hand for the clothes-brush.

II

The next morning, hearing nothing from Poirot, I went out for a stroll, met some old friends, and lunched with them at their hotel. In the afternoon we went for a spin. A punctured tyre delayed us, and it was past eight when I got back to the Grand Metropolitan.

The first sight that met my eyes was Poirot, looking even more diminutive than usual, sandwiched between the Opalsens, beaming in a state of placid satisfaction.

'*Mon ami* Hastings!' he cried, and sprang to meet me. 'Embrace me, my friend; all has marched to a marvel!'

Luckily, the embrace was merely figurative – not a thing one is always sure of with Poirot.

'Do you mean –' I began.

'Just wonderful, I call it!' said Mrs Opalsen, smiling all over her fat face. 'Didn't I tell you, Ed, that if he couldn't get back my pearls nobody would?'

'You did, my dear, you did. And you were right.'

I looked helplessly at Poirot, and he answered the glance.

'My friend Hastings is, as you say in England, all at the seaside. Seat yourself, and I will recount to you all the affair that has so happily ended.'

'Ended?'

'But yes. They are arrested.'

'Who are arrested?'

'The chambermaid and the valet, *parbleu*! You did not suspect? Not with my parting hint about the French chalk?'

'You said cabinet-makers used it.'

'Certainly they do – to make drawers slide easily. Somebody wanted the drawer to slide in and out without any noise. Who could that be? Obviously, only the chambermaid. The plan was so ingenious that it did not at once leap to the eye – not even to the eye of Hercule Poirot.

'Listen, this was how it was done. The valet was in the empty room next door, waiting. The French maid leaves the room. Quick as a flash the chambermaid whips open the drawer, takes out the jewel-case and, slipping back the bolt, passes it through the door. The valet opens it at his leisure with the duplicate key with which he has provided himself, extracts the necklace, and waits his time. Célestine leaves the room again, and – pst! – in a flash the case is passed back again and replaced in the drawer.

'Madame arrives, the theft is discovered. The chambermaid demands to be searched, with a good deal of righteous indignation, and leaves the room without a stain on her character. The imitation necklace with which they have provided themselves has been concealed in the French girl's bed that morning by the chambermaid – a master stroke, *ça*!'

'But what did you go to London for?'

'You remember the card?'

'Certainly. It puzzled me – and puzzles me still. I thought –'

I hesitated delicately, glancing at Mr Opalsen.

Poirot laughed heartily.

'*Une blague*! For the benefit of the valet. The card was one with a specially prepared surface – for finger-prints. I went straight to Scotland Yard, asked for our old friend Inspector Japp, and laid the facts before him. As I had suspected, the fingerprints proved to be those of two well-known jewel thieves who have been "wanted" for some time. Japp came down with me, the thieves were arrested, and the necklace was discovered in the valet's possession. A clever pair, but they failed in *method*. Have I not told you, Hastings, at least thirty-six times, that without method –'

'At least thirty-six thousand times!' I interrupted. 'But where did their "method" break down?'

'*Mon ami*, it is a good plan to take a place as chambermaid or valet – but you must not shirk your work. They left an empty room undusted; and therefore, when the man put down the jewel-case on the little table near the communicating door, it left a square mark –'

'I remember,' I cried.

'Before, I was undecided. Then – I *knew*!'

There was a moment's silence.

'And I've got my pearls,' said Mrs Opalsen as a sort of Greek chorus.

'Well,' I said, 'I'd better have some dinner.'

Poirot accompanied me.

'This ought to mean kudos for you,' I observed.

'*Pas du tout*,' replied Poirot tranquilly. 'Japp and the local inspector will divide the credit between them. But' – he tapped his pocket – 'I have a cheque here, from Mr Opalsen, and, how you say, my friend? This weekend has not gone according to plan. Shall we return here next weekend – at my expense this time?'

Part 8

The Kidnapped Prime Minister

Now that war and the problems of war are things of the past, I think I may safely venture to reveal to the world the part which my friend Poirot played in a moment of national crisis. The secret has been well guarded. Not a whisper of it reached the Press. But, now that the need for secrecy has gone by, I feel it is only just that England should know the debt it owes to my quaint little friend, whose marvellous brain so ably averted a great catastrophe.

One evening after dinner – I will not particularize the date; it suffices to say that it was at the time when 'Peace by negotiation' was the parrot-cry of England's enemies – my friend and I were sitting in his rooms. After being invalided out of the Army I had been given a recruiting job, and it had become my custom to drop in on Poirot in the evenings after dinner and talk with him of any cases of interest that he might have had on hand.

I was attempting to discuss with him the sensational news of the day – no less than an attempted assassination of Mr David MacAdam, England's Prime Minister. The account in the papers had evidently been carefully censored. No details were given, save that the Prime Minister had had a marvellous escape, the bullet just grazing his cheek.

I considered that our police must have been shamefully careless for such an outrage to be possible. I could well understand that the German agents in England would be willing to risk much for such an achievement. 'Fighting Mac', as his own party had nicknamed him, had strenuously and unequivocally combated the Pacifist influence which was becoming so prevalent.

He was more than England's Prime Minister – he *was* England; and to have removed him from his sphere of influence would have been a crushing and paralysing blow to Britain.

Poirot was busy mopping a grey suit with a minute sponge. Never was there a dandy such as Hercule Poirot. Neatness and order were his passion. Now, with the odour of benzene filling the air, he was quite unable to give me his full attention.

'In a little minute I am with you, my friend. I have all but finished. The spot of grease – he is not good – I remove him – so!' He waved his sponge.

I smiled as I lit another cigarette.

'Anything interesting on?' I inquired, after a minute or two.

'I assist a – how do you call it? – "charlady" to find her husband. A difficult affair, needing the tact. For I have a little idea that when he is found he will not be pleased. What would you? For my part, I sympathize with him. He was a man of discrimination to lose himself.'

I laughed.

'At last! The spot of grease, he is gone! I am at your disposal.'

'I was asking you what you thought of this attempt to assassinate MacAdam?'

'*Enfantillage!*' replied Poirot promptly. 'One can hardly take it seriously. To fire with the rifle – never does it succeed. It is a device of the past.'

'It was very near succeeding this time,' I reminded him.

Poirot shook his head impatiently. He was about to reply when the landlady thrust her head round the door and informed him that there were two gentlemen below who wanted to see him.

'They won't give their names, sir, but they says as it's very important.'

'Let them mount,' said Poirot, carefully folding his grey trousers.

In a few minutes the two visitors were ushered in, and my heart gave a leap as in the foremost I recognized no less a personage than Lord Estair, Leader of the House of Commons; whilst his companion, Mr Bernard Dodge, was also a member of the War Cabinet, and, as I knew, a close personal friend of the Prime Minister.

'Monsieur Poirot?' said Lord Estair interrogatively. My friend bowed. The great man looked at me and hesitated. 'My business is private.'

'You may speak freely before Captain Hastings,' said my friend, nodding to me to remain. 'He has not all the gifts, no! But I answer for his discretion.'

Lord Estair still hesitated, but Mr Dodge broke in abruptly:

'Oh, come on – don't let's beat about the bush! As far as I can see, the whole of England will know the hole we're in soon enough. Time's everything.'

'Pray be seated, messieurs,' said Poirot politely. 'Will you take the big chair, *milord*?'

Lord Estair started slightly. 'You know me?'

Poirot smiled. 'Certainly. I read the little papers with the pictures. How should I not know you?'

'Monsieur Poirot, I have come to consult you upon a matter of the most vital urgency. I must ask for absolute secrecy.'

'You have the word of Hercule Poirot – I can say no more!' said my friend grandiloquently.

'It concerns the Prime Minister. We are in grave trouble.'

'We're up a tree!' interposed Mr Dodge.

'The injury is serious then?' I asked.

'What injury?'

'The bullet wound.'

'Oh, that!' cried Mr Dodge contemptuously. 'That's old history.'

'As my colleague says,' continued Lord Estair, 'that affair is over and done with. Luckily, it failed. I wish I could say as much for the second attempt.'

'There has been a second attempt, then?'

'Yes, though not of the same nature, Monsieur Poirot, the Prime Minister has disappeared.'

'What?'

'He has been kidnapped!'

'Impossible!' I cried, stupefied.

Poirot threw a withering glance at me, which I knew enjoined me to keep my mouth shut.

'Unfortunately, impossible as it seems, it is only too true,' continued his lordship.

Poirot looked at Mr Dodge. 'You said just now, monsieur, that time was everything. What did you mean by that?'

The two men exchanged glances, and then Lord Estair said:

'You have heard, Monsieur Poirot, of the approaching Allied Conference?'

'My friend nodded.

'For obvious reasons, no details have been given of when and where it is to take place. But, although it has been kept out of the newspapers, the date is, of course, widely known in diplomatic circles. The Conference is to be held tomorrow – Thursday – evening at Versailles. Now you perceive the terrible gravity of the situation. I will not conceal from you that the Prime Minister's presence at the Conference is a vital necessity. The Pacifist propaganda, started and maintained by the German agents in our midst, has been very active. It is the universal opinion that the turning-point of the Conference will be the strong personality of the Prime Minister. His absence may have the most serious results – possibly a premature and disastrous peace. And we have no one who can be sent in his place. He alone can represent England.'

Poirot's face had grown very grave. 'Then you regard the kidnapping of the Prime Minister as a direct attempt to prevent his being present at the Conference?'

'Most certainly I do. He was actually on his way to France at the time.'

'And the Conference is to be held?'

'At nine o'clock tomorrow night.'

Poirot drew an enormous watch from his pocket.

'It is now a quarter to nine.'

'Twenty-four hours,' said Mr Dodge thoughtfully.

'And a quarter,' amended Poirot. 'Do not forget the quarter, monsieur – it may come in useful. Now for the details – the abduction, did it take place in England or in France?'

'In France. Mr MacAdam crossed to France this morning. He was to stay tonight as the guest of the Commander-in-Chief, proceeding tomorrow to Paris. He was conveyed across the Channel by destroyer. At Boulogne he was met by a car from General Headquarters and one of the Commander-in-Chief's ADCs.'

'*Eh bien?*'

'Well, they started from Boulogne – but they never arrived.'

'What?'

'Monsieur Poirot, it was a bogus car and a bogus ADC. The real car was found in a side road, with the chauffeur and the ADC neatly gagged and bound.'

'And the bogus car?'

'Is still at large.'

Poirot made a gesture of impatience. 'Incredible! Surely it cannot escape attention for long?'

'So we thought. It seemed merely a question of searching thoroughly. That part of France is under Military Law. We were convinced that the car could not go long unnoticed. The French police and our own

183

Scotland Yard men and the military are straining every nerve. It is, as you say, incredible – but nothing has been discovered!'

At that moment a tap came at the door, and a young officer entered with a heavily sealed envelope which he handed to Lord Estair.

'Just through from France, sir. I brought it on here, as you directed.'

The Minister tore it open eagerly, and uttered an exclamation. The officer withdrew.

'Here is news at last! This telegram has just been decoded. They have found the second car, also the secretary, Daniels, chloroformed, gagged, and bound, in an abandoned farm near C—. He remembers nothing, except something being pressed against his mouth and nose from behind, and struggling to free himself. The police are satisfied as to the genuineness of his statement.'

'And they have found nothing else?'

'No.'

'Not the Prime Minister's dead body? Then, there is hope. But it is strange. Why, after trying to shoot him this morning, are they now taking so much trouble to keep him alive?'

Dodge shook his head. 'One thing's quite certain. They're determined at all costs to prevent his attending the Conference.'

'If it is humanly possible, the Prime Minister shall be there. God grant it is not too late. Now, messieurs, recount to me everything – from the beginning. I must know about this shooting affair as well.'

'Last night, the Prime Minister, accompanied by one of his secretaries, Captain Daniels –'

'The same who accompanied him to France?'

'Yes. As I was saying, they motored down to Windsor, where the Prime Minister was granted an Audience. Early this morning he returned to town, and it was on the way that the attempted assassination took place.'

'One moment, if you please. Who is this Captain Daniels? You have his dossier?'

Lord Estair smiled. 'I thought you would ask me that. We do not know very much of him. He is of no particular family. He has served in the English Army, and is an extremely able secretary, being an exceptionally fine linguist. I believe he speaks seven languages. It is for that reason that the Prime Minister chose him to accompany him to France.'

'Has he any relatives in England?'

'Two aunts. A Mrs Everard, who lives at Hampstead, and a Miss Daniels, who lives near Ascot.'

'Ascot? That is near to Windsor, is it not?'

'That point has not been overlooked. But it has led to nothing.'

'You regard the Capitaine Daniels, then, as above suspicion?'

A shade of bitterness crept into Lord Estair's voice, as he replied:

'No, Monsieur Poirot. In these days, I should hesitate before I pronounced *anyone* above suspicion.'

'*Très bien*. Now I understand, *milord*, that the Prime Minister would, as a matter of course, be under vigilant police protection, which ought to render any assault upon him an impossibility?'

Lord Estair bowed his head. 'That is so. The Prime Minister's car was closely followed by another car containing detectives in plain clothes. Mr MacAdam knew nothing of these precautions. He is personally a most fearless man, and would be inclined to sweep them away arbitrarily. But, naturally, the police make their own arrangements. In fact, the Premier's chauffeur, O'Murphy, is a CID man.'

'O'Murphy? That is a name of Ireland, is it not so?'

'Yes, he is an Irishman.'

'From what part of Ireland?'

'County Clare, I believe.'

'*Tiens*! But proceed, *milord*.'

'The Premier started for London. The car was a closed one. He and Captain Daniels sat inside. The second car followed as usual. But, unluckily, for some unknown reason, the Prime Minister's car deviated from the main road –'

'At a point where the road curves?' interrupted Poirot.

'Yes – but how did you know?'

'Oh, *c'est évident!* Continue!'

'For some unknown reason,' continued Lord Estair, 'the Premier's car left the main road. The police car, unaware of the deviation, continued to keep to the high road. At a short distance down the unfrequented lane, the Prime Minister's car was suddenly held up by a band of masked men. The chauffeur –'

'That brave O'Murphy!' murmured Poirot thoughtfully.

'The chauffeur, momentarily taken aback, jammed on the brakes. The Prime Minister put his head out of the window. Instantly a shot rang out – then another. The first one grazed his cheek, the second, fortunately, went wide. The chauffeur, now realizing the danger, instantly forged straight ahead, scattering the band of men.'

'A near escape,' I ejaculated, with a shiver.

'Mr MacAdam refused to make any fuss over the slight wound he had received. He declared it was only a scratch. He stopped at a local cottage hospital, where it was dressed and bound up – he did not, of course, reveal his identity. He then drove, as per schedule, straight to Charing Cross, where a special train for Dover was awaiting him, and, after a brief account of what had happened had been given to the anxious police by Captain Daniels, he duly departed for France. At Dover, he went on board the waiting destroyer. At Boulogne, as you know, the bogus car was waiting for him, carrying the Union Jack, and correct in every detail.'

'That is all you have to tell me?'

'Yes.'

'There is no other circumstance that you have omitted, *milord*?'

'Well, there is one rather peculiar thing.'

'Yes?'

'The Prime Minister's car did not return home after leaving the Prime Minister at Charing Cross. The police were anxious to interview O'Murphy, so a search was instituted at once. The car was discovered standing outside a certain unsavoury little restaurant in Soho, which is well known as a meeting-place of German agents.'

'And the chauffeur?'

'The chauffeur was nowhere to be found. He, too, had disappeared.'

'So,' said Poirot thoughtfully, 'there are two disappearances: the Prime Minister in France, and O'Murphy in London.'

He looked keenly at Lord Estair, who made a gesture of despair.

'I can only tell you, Monsieur Poirot, that, if anyone had suggested to me yesterday that O'Murphy was a traitor, I should have laughed in his face.'

'And today?'

'Today I do not know what to think.'

Poirot nodded gravely. He looked at his turnip of a watch again.

'I understand that I have *carte blanche*, messieurs – in every way, I mean? I must be able to go where I choose, and how I choose.'

'Perfectly. There is a special train leaving for Dover in an hour's time, with a further contingent from Scotland Yard. You shall be accompanied by a Military officer and a CID man, who will hold themselves at your disposal in every way. Is that satisfactory?'

'Quite. One more question before you leave, messieurs. What made you come to me? I am unknown, obscure in this great London of yours.'

'We sought you out on the express recommendation and wish of a very great man of your own country.'

'*Comment*? My old friend the *Préfet* –?'

Lord Estair shook his head.

'One higher than the *Préfet*. One whose word was once law in Belgium – and shall be again! That England has sworn!'

Poirot's hand flew swiftly to a dramatic salute. 'Amen

189

to that! Ah, but my Master does not forget . . . Messieurs, I, Hercule Poirot, will serve you faithfully. Heaven only send that it will be in time. But this is dark – dark . . . I cannot see.'

'Well, Poirot,' I cried impatiently, as the door closed behind the Ministers, 'what do you think?'

My friend was busy packing a minute suitcase, with quick, deft movements. He shook his head thoughtfully.

'I don't know what to think. My brains desert me.'

'Why, as you said, kidnap him, when a knock on the head would do as well?' I mused.

'Pardon me, *mon ami,* but I did not quite say that. It is undoubtedly far more their affair to kidnap him.'

'But why?'

'Because uncertainty creates panic. That is one reason. Were the Prime Minister dead, it would be a terrible calamity, but the situation would have to be faced. But now you have paralysis. Will the Prime Minister reappear, or will he not? Is he dead or alive? Nobody knows, and until they know nothing definite can be done. And, as I tell you, uncertainty breeds panic, which is what *les Boches* are playing for. Then, again, if the kidnappers are holding him secretly somewhere, they have the advantage of being able to make terms with both sides. The German Government is not a liberal paymaster, as a rule, but no doubt they can be made to disgorge substantial remittances in such a case as this. Thirdly, they run no risk of the hangman's rope. Oh, decidedly, kidnapping is their affair.'

'Then, if that is so, why should they first try to shoot him?'

Poirot made a gesture of anger. 'Ah, that is just what I do not understand! It is inexplicable – stupid! They have all their arrangements made (and very good arrangements too!) for the abduction, and yet they imperil the whole affair by a melodramatic attack, worthy of a cinema, and quite as unreal. It is almost impossible to believe in it, with its band of masked men, not twenty miles from London!'

'Perhaps they were two quite separate attempts which happened irrespective of each other,' I suggested.

'Ah, no, that would be too much of a coincidence! Then, further – who is the traitor? There must have been a traitor – in the first affair, anyway. But who was it – Daniels or O'Murphy? It must have been one of the two, or why did the car leave the main road? We cannot suppose that the Prime Minister connived at his own assassination! Did O'Murphy take that turning of his own accord, or was it Daniels who told him to do so?'

'Surely it must have been O'Murphy's doing.'

'Yes, because if it was Daniels' the Prime Minister

Agatha Christie

would have heard the order, and would have asked the reason. But there are altogether too many "whys" in this affair, and they contradict each other. If O'Murphy is an honest man, *why* did he leave the main road? But if he was a dishonest man, *why* did he start the car again when only two shots had been fired – thereby, in all probability, saving the Prime Minister's life? And, again, if he was honest, why did he, immediately on leaving Charing Cross, drive to a well-known rendezvous of German spies?'

'It looks bad,' I said.

'Let us look at the case with method. What have we for and against these two men? Take O'Murphy first. Against: that his conduct in leaving the main road was suspicious; that he is an Irishman from County Clare; that he has disappeared in a highly suggestive manner. For: that his promptness in restarting the car saved the Premier's life; that he is a Scotland Yard man, and, obviously, from the post allotted to him, a trusted detective. Now for Daniels. There is not much against him, except the fact that nothing is known of his antecedents, and that he speaks too many languages for a good Englishman! (Pardon me, *mon ami*, but, as linguists, you are deplorable!) Now *for* him, we have the fact that he was found gagged, bound, and chloroformed – which does not look as though he had anything to do with the matter.'

'He might have gagged and bound himself, to divert suspicion.'

Poirot shook his head. 'The French police would make no mistake of that kind. Besides, once he had attained his object, and the Prime Minister was safely abducted, there would not be much point in his remaining behind. His accomplices *could* have gagged and chloroformed him, of course, but I fail to see what object they hoped to accomplish by it. He can be of little use to them now, for, until the circumstances concerning the Prime Minister have been cleared up, he is bound to be closely watched.'

'Perhaps he hoped to start the police on a false scent?'

'Then why did he not do so? He merely says that something was pressed over his nose and mouth, and that he remembers nothing more. There is no false scent there. It sounds remarkably like the truth.'

'Well,' I said, glancing at the clock, 'I suppose we'd better start for the station. You may find more clues in France.'

'Possibly, *mon ami*, but I doubt it. It is still incredible to me that the Prime Minister has not been discovered in that limited area, where the difficulty of concealing him must be tremendous. If the military and the police of two countries have not found him, how shall I?'

Agatha Christie

At Charing Cross we were met by Mr Dodge.

'This is Detective Barnes, of Scotland Yard, and Major Norman. They will hold themselves entirely at your disposal. Good luck to you. It's a bad business, but I've not given up hope. Must be off now.' And the Minister strode rapidly away.

We chatted in a desultory fashion with Major Norman. In the centre of the little group of men on the platform I recognized a little ferret-faced fellow talking to a tall, fair man. He was an old acquaintance of Poirot's – Detective-Inspector Japp, supposed to be one of the smartest of Scotland Yard's officers. He came over and greeted my friend cheerfully.

'I heard you were on this job too. Smart bit of work. So far they've got away with the goods all right. But I can't believe they can keep him hidden long. Our people are going through France with a toothcomb. So are the French. I can't help feeling it's only a matter of hours now.'

'That is, if he's still alive,' remarked the tall detective gloomily.

Japp's face fell. 'Yes . . . but somehow I've got the feeling he's still alive all right.'

Poirot nodded. 'Yes, yes; he's alive. But can he be found in time? I, like you, did not believe he could be hidden so long.'

The whistle blew, and we all trooped up into the

Pullman car. Then, with a slow, unwilling jerk, the train drew out of the station.

It was a curious journey. The Scotland Yard men crowded together. Maps of Northern France were spread out, and eager forefingers traced the lines of roads and villages. Each man had his own pet theory. Poirot showed none of his usual loquacity, but sat staring in front of him, with an expression on his face that reminded me of a puzzled child. I talked to Norman, whom I found quite an amusing fellow. On arriving at Dover Poirot's behaviour moved me to intense amusement. The little man, as he went on board the boat, clutched desperately at my arm. The wind was blowing lustily.

'*Mon Dieu!*' he murmured. 'This is terrible!'

'Have courage, Poirot,' I cried. 'You will succeed. You will find him. I am sure of it.'

'Ah, *mon ami*, you mistake my emotion. It is this villainous sea that troubles me! The *mal de mer* – it is horrible suffering!'

'Oh!' I said, rather taken aback.

The first throb of the engines was felt, and Poirot groaned and closed his eyes.

'Major Norman has a map of Northern France if you would like to study it?'

Poirot shook his head impatiently.

'But no, but no! Leave me, my friend. See you, to

think, the stomach and the brain must be in harmony. Laverguier has a method most excellent for averting the *mal de mer*. You breathe in – and out – slowly, so – turning the head from left to right and counting six between each breath.'

I left him to his gymnastic endeavours, and went on deck.

As we came slowly into Boulogne Harbour Poirot appeared, neat and smiling, and announced to me in a whisper that Laverguier's system had succeeded 'to a marvel!'

Japp's forefinger was still tracing imaginary routes on his map. 'Nonsense! The car started from Boulogne – here they branched off. Now, my idea is that they transferred the Prime Minister to another car. See?'

'Well,' said the tall detective, 'I shall make for the seaports. Ten to one, they've smuggled him on board a ship.'

Japp shook his head. 'Too obvious. The order went out at once to close all the ports.'

The day was just breaking as we landed. Major Norman touched Poirot on the arm. 'There's a military car here waiting for you, sir.'

'Thank you, monsieur. But, for the moment, I do not propose to leave Boulogne.'

'What?'

'No, we will enter this hotel here, by the quay.'

He suited the action to the word, demanded and was accorded a private room. We three followed him, puzzled and uncomprehending.

He shot a quick glance at us. 'It is not so that the good detective should act, eh? I perceive your thought. He must be full of energy. He must rush to and fro. He should prostrate himself on the dusty road and seek the marks of tyres through a little glass. He must gather up the cigarette-end, the fallen match? That is your idea, is it not?'

His eyes challenged us. 'But I – Hercule Poirot – tell you that it is not so! The true clues are within – *here!*' He tapped his forehead. 'See you, I need not have left London. It would have been sufficient for me to sit quietly in my rooms there. All that matters is the little grey cells within. Secretly and silently they do their part, until suddenly I call for a map, and I lay my finger on a spot – so – and I say: the Prime Minister is *there!* And it is so! With method and logic one can accomplish anything! This frantic rushing to France was a mistake – it is playing a child's game of hide-and-seek. But now, though it may be too late, I will set to work the right way, from within. Silence, my friends, I beg of you.'

And for five long hours the little man sat motionless, blinking his eyelids like a cat, his green eyes flickering and becoming steadily greener and greener.

Agatha Christie

The Scotland Yard man was obviously contemptuous, Major Norman was bored and impatient, and I myself found the time passed with wearisome slowness.

Finally, I got up, and strolled as noiselessly as I could to the window. The matter was becoming a farce. I was secretly concerned for my friend. If he failed, I would have preferred him to fail in a less ridiculous manner. Out of the window I idly watched the daily leave boat, belching forth columns of smoke, as she lay alongside the quay.

Suddenly I was aroused by Poirot's voice close to my elbow.

'*Mes amis*, let us start!'

I turned. An extraordinary transformation had come over my friend. His eyes were flickering with excitement, his chest was swelled to the uttermost.

'I have been an imbecile, my friends! But I see daylight at last.'

Major Norman moved hastily to the door. 'I'll order the car.'

'There is no need. I shall not use it. Thank Heaven the wind has fallen.'

'Do you mean you are going to walk, sir?'

'No, my young friend. I am no St Peter. I prefer to cross the sea by boat.'

'To cross the *sea*?'

'Yes. To work with method, one must begin from

the beginning. And the beginning of this affair was in England. Therefore, we return to England.'

II

At three o'clock, we stood once more upon Charing Cross platform. To all our expostulations, Poirot turned a deaf ear, and reiterated again and again that to start at the beginning was not a waste of time, but the only way. On the way over, he had conferred with Norman in a low voice, and the latter had despatched a sheaf of telegrams from Dover.

Owing to the special passes held by Norman, we got through everywhere in record time. In London, a large police car was waiting for us, with some plain-clothes men, one of whom handed a typewritten sheet of paper to my friend. He answered my inquiring glance.

'A list of the cottage hospitals within a certain radius west of London. I wired for it from Dover.'

We were whirled rapidly through the London streets. We were on the Bath Road. On we went, through Hammersmith, Chiswick and Brentford. I began to see our objective. Through Windsor and so on to Ascot. My heart gave a leap. Ascot was where Daniels had an aunt living. We were after *him*, then, not O'Murphy.

Agatha Christie

We duly stopped at the gate of a trim villa. Poirot jumped out and rang the bell. I saw a perplexed frown dimming the radiance of his face. Plainly, he was not satisfied. The bell was answered. He was ushered inside. In a few moments he reappeared, and climbed into the car with a short, sharp shake of his head. My hopes began to die down. It was past four now. Even if he found certain evidence incriminating Daniels, what would be the good of it, unless he could wring from someone the exact spot in France where they were holding the Prime Minister?

Our return progress towards London was an interrupted one. We deviated from the main road more than once, and occasionally stopped at a small building, which I had no difficulty in recognizing as a cottage hospital. Poirot only spent a few minutes at each, but at every halt his radiant assurance was more and more restored.

He whispered something to Norman, to which the latter replied:

'Yes, if you turn off to the left, you will find them waiting by the bridge.'

We turned up a side road, and in the failing light I discerned a second car, waiting by the side of the road. It contained two men in plain clothes. Poirot got down and spoke to them, and then we started off in a northerly direction, the other car following close behind.

We drove for some time, our objective being obviously one of the northern suburbs of London. Finally, we drove up to the front door of a tall house, standing a little back from the road in its own grounds.

Norman and I were left in the car. Poirot and one of the detectives went up to the door and rang. A neat parlourmaid opened it. The detective spoke.

'I am a police officer, and I have a warrant to search this house.'

The girl gave a little scream, and a tall, handsome woman of middle age appeared behind her in the hall.

'Shut the door, Edith. They are burglars, I expect.'

But Poirot swiftly inserted his foot in the door, and at the same moment blew a whistle. Instantly the other detectives ran up, and poured into the house, shutting the door behind them.

Norman and I spent about five minutes cursing our forced inactivity. Finally the door reopened, and the men emerged, escorting three prisoners – a woman and two men. The woman, and one of the men, were taken to the second car. The other man was placed in our car by Poirot himself.

'I must go with the others, my friend. But have great care of this gentleman. You do not know him, no? *Eh bien*, let me present to you, Monsieur O'Murphy!'

O'Murphy! I *gaped* at him open-mouthed as we

started again. He was not handcuffed, but I did not fancy he would try to escape. He sat there staring in front of him as though dazed. Anyway, Norman and I would be more than a match for him.

To my surprise, we still kept a northerly route. We were not returning to London, then! I was much puzzled. Suddenly, as the car slowed down, I recognized that we were close to Hendon Aerodrome. Immediately I grasped Poirot's idea. He proposed to reach France by aeroplane.

It was a sporting idea, but, on the face of it, impracticable. A telegram would be far quicker. Time was everything. He must leave the personal glory of rescuing the Prime Minister to others.

As we drew up, Major Norman jumped out, and a plainclothes man took his place. He conferred with Poirot for a few minutes, and then went off briskly.

I, too, jumped out, and caught Poirot by the arm.

'I congratulate you, old fellow! They have told you the hiding-place? But, look here, you must wire to France at once. You'll be too late if you go yourself.'

Poirot looked at me curiously for a minute or two.

'Unfortunately, my friend, there are some things that cannot be sent by telegram.'

III

At that moment Major Norman returned, accompanied by a young officer in the uniform of the Flying Corps.

'This is Captain Lyall, who will fly you over to France. He can start at once.'

'Wrap up warmly, sir,' said the young pilot. 'I can lend you a coat, if you like.'

Poirot was consulting his enormous watch. He murmured to himself: 'Yes, there is time – just time.' Then he looked up and bowed politely to the young officer. 'I thank you, monsieur. But it is not I who am your passenger. It is this gentleman here.'

He moved a little aside as he spoke, and a figure came forward out of the darkness. It was the second male prisoner who had gone in the other car, and as the light fell on his face, I gave a start of surprise.

It was the Prime Minister!

IV

'For Heaven's sake, tell me all about it,' I cried impatiently, as Poirot, Norman and I motored back to London. 'How in the world did they manage to smuggle him back to England?'

'There was no need to smuggle him back,' replied Poirot dryly. 'The Prime Minister has never left England. He was kidnapped on his way from Windsor to London.'

'*What?*'

'I will make all clear. The Prime Minister was in his car, his secretary beside him. Suddenly a pad of chloroform is clapped on his face –'

'But by whom?'

'By the clever linguistic Captain Daniels. As soon as the Prime Minister is unconscious, Daniels picks up the speaking-tube, and directs O'Murphy to turn to the right, which the chauffeur, quite unsuspicious, does. A few yards down that unfrequented road a large car is standing, apparently broken down. Its driver signals to O'Murphy to stop. O'Murphy slows up. The stranger approaches. Daniels leans out of the window, and, probably with the aid of an instantaneous anaesthetic, such as ethylchloride, the chloroform trick is repeated. In a few seconds, the two helpless men are dragged out and transferred to the other car, and a pair of substitutes take their places.'

'Impossible!'

'*Pas du tout!* Have you not seen music-hall turns imitating celebrities with marvellous accuracy? Nothing is easier than to personate a public character. The Prime Minister of England is far easier to understudy than Mr John Smith of Clapham, say. As for O'Murphy's "double", no one was going to take much notice of him until after the departure of the Prime Minister, and by then he would have made himself scarce. He drives straight from Charing Cross to the meeting-place of his friends. He goes in as O'Murphy, he emerges as someone quite different. O'Murphy has disappeared, leaving a conveniently suspicious trail behind him.'

'But the man who personated the Prime Minister was seen by everyone!'

'He was not seen by anyone who knew him privately or intimately. And Daniels shielded him from contact with anyone as much as possible. Moreover, his face was bandaged up, and anything unusual in his manner would be put down to the fact that he was suffering from shock as a result of the attempt upon his life. Mr MacAdam has a weak throat, and always spares his voice as much as possible before any great speech. The deception was perfectly easy to keep up as far as France. There it would be impracticable and impossible – so the Prime Minister disappears. The police of this country hurry across the Channel, and no one bothers to go into the details of the first attack. To sustain the illusion that the abduction has taken place in France, Daniels is gagged and chloroformed in a convincing manner.'

'And the man who has enacted the part of the Prime Minister?'

'Rids himself of his disguise. He and the bogus chauffeur may be arrested as suspicious characters, but no one will dream of suspecting their real part in the drama, and they will eventually be released for lack of evidence.'

'And the real Prime Minister?'

'He and O'Murphy were driven straight to the house of "Mrs Everard", at Hampstead, Daniels' so-called "aunt". In reality, she is Frau Bertha Ebenthal, and the police have been looking for her for some time. It is a valuable little present that I have made them – to say nothing of Daniels! Ah, it was a clever plan, but he did not reckon on the cleverness of Hercule Poirot!'

I think my friend might well be excused his moment of vanity.

'When did you first begin to suspect the truth of the matter?'

'When I began to work the right way – from *within*! I could not make that shooting affair fit in – but when I saw that the net result of it was that *the Prime Minister went to France with his face bound up* I began to comprehend! And when I visited all the cottage hospitals between Windsor and London, and found that no one answering to my description had had his face bound up and dressed that morning, I was sure! After that, it was child's play for a mind like mine!'

The following morning, Poirot showed me a telegram he had just received. It had no place of origin, and was unsigned. It ran:

'In time.'

Later in the day the evening papers published an account of the Allied Conference. They laid particular stress on the magnificent ovation accorded to Mr David MacAdam, whose inspiring speech had produced a deep and lasting impression.

Part 9

The Disappearance
of Mr Davenheim

Poirot and I were expecting our old friend Inspector Japp of Scotland Yard to tea. We were sitting round the tea-table awaiting his arrival. Poirot had just finished carefully straightening the cups and saucers which our landlady was in the habit of throwing, rather than placing, on the table. He had also breathed heavily on the metal teapot, and polished it with a silk handkerchief. The kettle was on the boil, and a small enamel saucepan beside it contained some thick, sweet chocolate which was more to Poirot's palate than what he described as 'your English poison'.

A sharp 'rat-tat' sounded below, and a few minutes afterwards Japp entered briskly.

'Hope I'm not late,' he said as he greeted us. 'To tell the truth, I was yarning with Miller, the man who's in charge of the Davenheim case.'

I pricked up my ears. For the last three days the

Agatha Christie

papers had been full of the strange disappearance of Mr Davenheim, senior partner of Davenheim and Salmon, the well-known bankers and financiers. On Saturday last he had walked out of his house, and had never been seen since. I looked forward to extracting some interesting details from Japp.

'I should have thought,' I remarked, 'that it would be almost impossible for anyone to "disappear" nowadays.'

Poirot moved a plate of bread and butter the eighth of an inch, and said sharply:

'Be exact, my friend. What do you mean by "disappear"? To which class of disappearance are you referring?'

'Are disappearances classified and labelled, then?' I laughed.

Japp smiled also. Poirot frowned at both of us.

'But certainly they are! They fall into three categories: First, and most common, the voluntary disappearance. Second, the much abused "loss of memory" case – rare, but occasionally genuine. Third, murder, and a more or less successful disposal of the body. Do you refer to all three as impossible of execution?'

'Very nearly so, I should think. You might lose your own memory, but someone would be sure to recognize you – especially in the case of a well-known man like Davenheim. Then "bodies" can't be made to vanish

210

into thin air. Sooner or later they turn up, concealed in lonely places, or in trunks. Murder will out. In the same way, the absconding clerk, or the domestic defaulter, is bound to be run down in these days of wireless telegraphy. He can be headed off from foreign countries; ports and railway stations are watched; and as for concealment in this country, his features and appearance will be known to everyone who reads a daily newspaper. He's up against civilization.'

'*Mon ami*,' said Poirot, 'you make one error. You do not allow for the fact that a man who had decided to make away with another man – or with himself in a figurative sense – might be that rare machine, a man of method. He might bring intelligence, talent, a careful calculation of detail to the task; and then I do not see why he should not be successful in baffling the police force.'

'But not *you*, I suppose?' said Japp good-humouredly, winking at me. 'He couldn't baffle you, eh, Monsieur Poirot?'

Poirot endeavoured, with a marked lack of success, to look modest. 'Me also! Why not? It is true that I approach such problems with an exact science, a mathematical precision, which seems, alas, only too rare in the new generation of detectives!'

Japp grinned more widely.

'I don't know,' he said. 'Miller, the man who's on

this case, is a smart chap. You may be very sure he won't overlook a footprint, or a cigar-ash, or a crumb even. He's got eyes that see everything.'

'So, *mon ami*,' said Poirot, 'has the London sparrow. But all the same, I should not ask the little brown bird to solve the problem of Mr Davenheim.'

'Come now, monsieur, you're not going to run down the value of details as clues?'

'By no means. These things are all good in their way. The danger is they may assume undue importance. Most details are insignificant; one or two are vital. It is the brain, the little grey cells' – he tapped his forehead – 'on which one must rely. The senses mislead. One must seek the truth within – not without.'

'You don't mean to say, Monsieur Poirot, that you would undertake to solve a case without moving from your chair, do you?'

'That is exactly what I do mean – granted the facts were placed before me. I regard myself as a consulting specialist.'

Japp slapped his knee. 'Hanged if I don't take you at your word. Bet you a fiver that you can't lay your hand – or rather tell me where to lay my hand – on Mr Davenheim, dead or alive, before a week is out.'

Poirot considered. '*Eh bien, mon ami*, I accept. *Le sport*, it is the passion of you English. Now – the facts.'

'On Saturday last, as is his usual custom, Mr Davenheim took the 12.40 train from Victoria to Chingside, where his palatial country seat, The Cedars, is situated. After lunch, he strolled round the grounds, and gave various directions to the gardeners. Everybody agrees that his manner was absolutely normal and as usual. After tea he put his head into his wife's boudoir, saying that he was going to stroll down to the village and post some letters. He added that he was expecting a Mr Lowen, on business. If he should come before he himself returned, he was to be shown into the study and asked to wait. Mr Davenheim then left the house by the front door, passed leisurely down the drive, and out at the gate, and – was never seen again. From that hour, he vanished completely.'

'Pretty – very pretty – altogether a charming little problem,' murmured Poirot. 'Proceed, my good friend.'

'About a quarter of an hour later a tall, dark man with a thick black moustache rang the front door-bell, and explained that he had an appointment with Mr Davenheim. He gave the name of Lowen, and in accordance with the banker's instructions was shown into the study. Nearly an hour passed. Mr Davenheim did not return. Finally Mr Lowen rang the bell, and explained that he was unable to wait any longer, as he must catch his train back to town.

Agatha Christie

Mrs Davenheim apologized for her husband's absence, which seemed unaccountable, as she knew him to have been expecting the visitor. Mr Lowen reiterated his regrets and took his departure.

'Well, as everyone knows, Mr Davenheim did *not* return. Early on Sunday morning the police were communicated with, but could make neither head nor tail of the matter. Mr Davenheim seemed literally to have vanished into thin air. He had not been to the post office; nor had he been seen passing through the village. At the station they were positive he had not departed by any train. His own motor had not left the garage. If he had hired a car to meet him in some lonely spot, it seems almost certain that by this time, in view of the large reward offered for information, the driver of it would have come forward to tell what he knew. True, there was a small race-meeting at Entfield, five miles away, and if he had walked to that station he might have passed unnoticed in the crowd. But since then his photograph and a full description of him have been circulated in every newspaper, and nobody has been able to give any news of him. We have, of course, received many letters from all over England, but each clue, so far, has ended in disappointment.

'On Monday morning a further sensational discovery came to light. Behind a *portière* in Mr Davenheim's study stands a safe, and that safe had been broken into and rifled. The windows were fastened securely on the inside, which seems to put an ordinary burglary out of court, unless, of course, an accomplice within the house fastened them again afterwards. On the other hand, Sunday having intervened, and the household being in a state of chaos, it is likely that the burglary was committed on the Saturday, and remained undetected until Monday.'

'*Précisément*,' said Poirot dryly. 'Well, is he arrested, *ce pauvre M Lowen?*'

Japp grinned. 'Not yet. But he's under pretty close supervision.'

Poirot nodded. 'What was taken from the safe? Have you any idea?'

'We've been going into that with the junior partner of the firm and Mrs Davenheim. Apparently there was a considerable amount in bearer bonds, and a very large sum in notes, owing to some large transaction having been just carried through. There was also a small fortune in jewellery. All Mrs Davenheim's jewels were kept in the safe. The purchasing of them had become a passion with her husband of late years, and hardly a month passed that he did not make her a present of some rare and costly gem.'

'Altogether a good haul,' said Poirot thoughtfully. 'Now, what about Lowen? Is it known what his business was with Davenheim that evening?'

'Well, the two men were apparently not on very good terms. Lowen is a speculator in quite a small way. Nevertheless, he has been able once or twice to score a coup off Davenheim in the market, though it seems they seldom or never actually met. It was a matter concerning some South American shares which led the banker to make his appointment.'

'Had Davenheim interests in South America, then?'

'I believe so. Mrs Davenheim happened to mention that he spent all last autumn in Buenos Aires.'

'Any trouble in his home life? Were the husband and wife on good terms?'

'I should say his domestic life was quite peaceful and uneventful. Mrs Davenheim is a pleasant, rather unintelligent woman. Quite a nonentity, I think.'

'Then we must not look for the solution of the mystery there. Had he any enemies?'

'He had plenty of financial rivals, and no doubt there are many people whom he has got the better of who bear him no particular goodwill. But there was no one likely to make away with him – and, if they had, where is the body?'

'Exactly. As Hastings says, bodies have a habit of coming to light with fatal persistency.'

'By the way, one of the gardeners says he saw a figure going round to the side of the house towards the rose-garden. The long french window of the study opens on to the rose-garden, and Mr Davenheim frequently entered and left the house that way. But the man was a good way off, at work on some cucumber frames, and cannot even say whether it was the figure of his master or not. Also, he cannot fix the time with any accuracy. It must have been before six, as the gardeners cease work at that time.'

'And Mr Davenheim left the house?'

'About half-past five or thereabouts.'

'What lies beyond the rose-garden?'

'A lake.'

'With a boathouse?'

'Yes, a couple of punts are kept there. I suppose you're thinking of suicide, Monsieur Poirot? Well, I don't mind telling you that Miller's going down tomorrow expressly to see that piece of water dragged. That's the kind of man he is!'

Poirot smiled faintly, and turned to me. 'Hastings, I pray you, hand me that copy of *Daily Megaphone*. If I remember rightly, there is an unusually clear photograph there of the missing man.'

I rose, and found the sheet required. Poirot studied the features attentively.

'H'm!' he murmured. 'Wears his hair rather long and wavy, full moustache and pointed beard, bushy eyebrows. Eyes dark?'

'Yes.'

'Hair and beard turning grey?'

The detective nodded. 'Well, Monsieur Poirot, what have you got to say to it all? Clear as daylight, eh?'

'On the contrary, most obscure.'

The Scotland Yard man looked pleased.

'Which gives me great hopes of solving it,' finished Poirot placidly.

'Eh?'

'I find it a good sign when a case is obscure. If a thing is clear as daylight – *eh bien*, mistrust it! Someone has made it so.'

Japp shook his head almost pityingly. 'Well, each to their fancy. But it's not a bad thing to see your way clear ahead.'

'I do not see,' murmured Poirot. 'I shut my eyes – and think.'

Japp sighed. 'Well, you've got a clear week to think in.'

'And you will bring me any fresh developments that arise – the result of the labours of the hard-working and lynx-eyed Inspector Miller, for instance?'

'Certainly. That's in the bargain.'

'Seems a shame, doesn't it?' said Japp to me as I accompanied him to the door. 'Like robbing a child!'

I could not help agreeing with a smile. I was still smiling as I re-entered the room.

'*Eh bien!*' said Poirot immediately. 'You make fun

of Papa Poirot, is it not so?' He shook his finger at me. 'You do not trust his grey cells? Ah, do not be confused! Let us discuss this little problem – incomplete as yet, I admit, but already showing one or two points of interest.'

'The lake!' I said significantly.

'And even more than the lake, the boathouse!'

I looked sidewise at Poirot. He was smiling in his most inscrutable fashion. I felt that, for the moment, it would be quite useless to question him further.

We heard nothing of Japp until the following evening, when he walked in about nine o'clock. I saw at once by his expression that he was bursting with news of some kind.

'*Eh bien*, my friend,' remarked Poirot. 'All goes well? But do not tell me that you have discovered the body of Mr Davenheim in your lake, because I shall not believe you.'

'We haven't found the body, but we did find his *clothes* – the identical clothes he was wearing that day. What do you say to that?'

'Any other clothes missing from the house?'

'No, his valet was quite positive on that point. The rest of his wardrobe is intact. There's more. We've arrested Lowen. One of the maids, whose business it is to fasten the bedroom windows, declares that she saw Lowen coming *towards* the study through the rose-garden about a quarter past six. That would be about ten minutes before he left the house.'

'What does he himself say to that?'

'Denied first of all that he had ever left the study. But the maid was positive, and he pretended afterwards that he had forgotten just stepping out of the window to examine an unusual species of rose. Rather a weak story! And there's fresh evidence against him come to light. Mr Davenheim always wore a thick gold ring set with a solitaire diamond on the little finger of his right hand. Well, that ring was pawned in London on Saturday night by a man called Billy Kellett! He's already known to the police – did three months last autumn for lifting an old gentleman's watch. It seems he tried to pawn the ring at no less than five different places, succeeded at the last one, got gloriously drunk on the proceeds, assaulted a policeman, and was run in in consequence. I went to Bow Street with Miller and saw him. He's sober enough now, and I don't mind admitting we pretty well frightened the life out of him, hinting he might be charged with murder. This is his yarn, and a very queer one it is.

'He was at Entfield races on Saturday, though I dare say scarfpins was his line of business, rather than betting. Anyway, he had a bad day, and was down on his luck. He was tramping along the road to Chingside, and sat down in a ditch to rest just before he got into the village. A few minutes later he noticed a man coming along the road to the village, "dark-complexioned gent, with a big moustache, one of them city toffs," is his description of the man.

'Kellett was half concealed from the road by a heap of stones. Just before he got abreast of him, the man looked quickly up and down the road, and seeing it apparently deserted he took a small object from his pocket and threw it over the hedge. Then he went on towards the station. Now, the object he had thrown over the hedge had fallen with a slight "chink" which aroused the curiosity of the human derelict in the ditch. He investigated and, after a short search, discovered the ring! That is Kellett's story. It's only fair to say that Lowen denies it utterly, and of course the word of a man like Kellett can't be relied upon in the slightest. It's within the bounds of possibility that he met Davenheim in the lane and robbed and murdered him.'

Poirot shook his head.

'Very improbable, *mon ami*. He had no means of disposing of the body. It would have been found by now. Secondly, the open way in which he pawned the ring makes it unlikely that he did murder to get it. Thirdly, your sneak-thief is rarely a murderer. Fourthly, as he has been in prison since Saturday, it would be too much of a coincidence that he is able to give so accurate a description of Lowen.'

Japp nodded. 'I don't say you're not right. But all the same, you won't get a jury to take much note of a jail-bird's evidence. What seems odd to me is that Lowen couldn't find a cleverer way of disposing of the ring.'

Poirot shrugged his shoulders. 'Well, after all, if it were found in the neighbourhood, it might be argued that Davenheim himself had dropped it.'

'But why remove it from the body at all?' I cried.

'There might be a reason for that,' said Japp. 'Do you know that just beyond the lake, a little gate leads out on to the hill, and not three minutes' walk brings you to – what do you think? – a *lime kiln*.'

'Good heavens!' I cried. 'You mean that the lime which destroyed the body would be powerless to affect the metal of the ring?'

'Exactly.'

'It seems to me,' I said, 'that that explains everything. What a horrible crime!'

By common consent we both turned and looked at Poirot. He seemed lost in reflection, his brow knitted, as though with some supreme mental effort. I felt at last his keen intellect was asserting itself. What would his first words be? We were not long left in doubt. With a sigh, the tension of his attitude relaxed and turning to Japp, he asked:

'Have you any idea, my friend, whether Mr and Mrs Davenheim occupied the same bedroom?'

The question seemed so ludicrously inappropriate that for a moment we both stared in silence. Then Japp burst into a laugh. 'Good Lord, Monsieur Poirot, I thought you were coming out with something startling. As to your question, I'm sure I don't know.'

'You could find out?' asked Poirot with curious persistence.

'Oh, certainly – if you *really* want to know.'

'*Merci, mon ami.* I should be obliged if you would make a point of it.'

Japp stared at him a few minutes longer, but Poirot seemed to have forgotten us both. The detective shook his head sadly at me, and murmuring, 'Poor old fellow! War's been too much for him!' gently withdrew from the room.

As Poirot seemed sunk in a daydream, I took a sheet of paper, and amused myself by scribbling notes upon it. My friend's voice aroused me. He had come out of his reverie, and was looking brisk and alert.

'*Que faites-vous là, mon ami?*'

'I was jotting down what occurred to me as the main points of interest in this affair.'

'You become methodical – at last!' said Poirot approvingly.

I concealed my pleasure. 'Shall I read them to you?'

'By all means.'

I cleared my throat.

'"One: All the evidence points to Lowen having been the man who forced the safe.

'"Two: He had a grudge against Davenheim.

'"Three: He lied in his first statement that he had never left the study.

'"Four: If you accept Billy Kellett's story as true, Lowen is unmistakably implicated."'

I paused. 'Well?' I asked, for I felt that I had put my finger on all the vital facts.

Poirot looked at me pityingly, shaking his head very gently. '*Mon pauvre ami!* But it is that you have not the gift! The important detail, you appreciate him never! Also, your reasoning is false.'

'How?'

'Let me take your four points.'

'One: Mr Lowen could not possibly know that he would have the chance to open the safe. He came for a business interview. He could not know beforehand that Mr Davenheim would be absent posting a letter, and that he would consequently be alone in the study!'

'He might have seized the opportunity,' I suggested.

'And the tools? City gentlemen do not carry round housebreaker's tools on the off chance! And one could not cut into that safe with penknife, *bien entendu!*'

'Well, what about Number Two?'

'You say Lowen had a grudge against Mr Davenheim. What you mean is that he had once or twice got the better of him. And presumably those transactions were entered into with the view of benefiting himself. In any case you do not as a rule bear a grudge against a man you have got the better of – it is more likely to be the other way about. Whatever grudge there might have been would have been on Mr Davenheim's side.'

'Well, you can't deny that he lied about never having left the study?'

'No. But he may have been frightened. Remember, the missing man's clothes had just been discovered in the lake. Of course, as usual, he would have done better to speak the truth.'

'And the fourth point?'

'I grant you that. If Kellett's story is true, Lowen is undeniably implicated. That is what makes the affair so very interesting.'

'Then I *did* appreciate one vital fact?'

'Perhaps – but you have entirely overlooked the two most important points, the ones which undoubtedly hold the clue to the whole matter.'

'And pray, what are they?'

'One, the passion which has grown upon Mr Davenheim in the last few years for buying jewellery. Two, his trip to Buenos Aires last autumn.'

'Poirot, you are joking?'

'I am serious. Ah, sacred thunder, but I hope Japp will not forget my little commission.'

Agatha Christie

But the detective, entering into the spirit of the joke, had remembered it so well that a telegram was handed to Poirot about eleven o'clock the next day. At his request I opened it and read it out:

"'Husband and wife have occupied separate rooms since last winter.'"

'Aha!' cried Poirot. 'And now we are in mid June! All is solved!'

I stared at him.

'You have no moneys in the bank of Davenheim and Salmon, *mon ami?*'

'No,' I said wondering. 'Why?'

'Because I should advise you to withdraw it – before it is too late.'

'Why, what do you expect?'

'I expect a big smash in a few days – perhaps sooner. Which reminds me, we will return the compliment of a *dépêche* to Japp. A pencil, I pray you, and a form. *Voilà!* 'Advise you to withdraw any money deposited with firm in question.' That will intrigue him, the good Japp! His eyes will open wide – wide! He will not comprehend in the slightest – until tomorrow, or the next day!'

I remained sceptical, but the morrow forced me to render tribute to my friend's remarkable powers.

In every paper was a huge headline telling of the sensational failure of the Davenheim bank. The disappearance of the famous financier took on a totally different aspect in the light of the revelation of the financial affairs of the bank.

Before we were half-way through breakfast, the door flew open and Japp rushed in. In his left hand was a paper; in his right was Poirot's telegram, which he banged down on the table in front of my friend.

'How did you know, Monsieur Poirot? How the blazes could you know?'

Poirot smiled placidly at him. 'Ah, *mon ami*, after your wire, it was a certainty! From the commencement, see you, it struck me that the safe burglary was somewhat remarkable. Jewels, ready money, bearer bonds – all so conveniently arranged for – whom? Well, the good Monsieur Davenheim was of those who "look after Number One" as your saying goes! It seemed almost certain that it was arranged for – himself! Then his passion of late years for buying jewellery! How simple! The funds he embezzled, he converted into jewels, very likely replacing them in turn with paste duplicates, and so he put away in a safe place, under another name, a considerable fortune to be enjoyed all in good time when everyone has been thrown off the track. His arrangements completed, he makes an appointment with Mr Lowen (who has been imprudent enough in the past to cross the great man once or twice), drills a hole in the safe, leaves orders that the guest is to be shown into the study, and walks out of the house – where?' Poirot stopped, and stretched out his hand for another boiled egg. He frowned. 'It is really insupportable,' he murmured, 'that every hen lays an egg of a different size! What symmetry can there be on the breakfast table? At least they should sort them in dozens at the shop!'

'Never mind the eggs,' said Japp impatiently. 'Let 'em lay 'em square if they like. Tell us where our customer went to when he left The Cedars – that is, if you know!'

'*Eh bien*, he went to his hiding place. Ah, this Monsieur Davenheim, there may be some malformation in his grey cells, but they are of the first quality!'

'Do you know where he is hiding?'

'Certainly! It is most ingenious.'

'For the Lord's sake, tell us, then!'

Poirot gently collected every fragment of shell from his plate, placed them in the egg-cup, and reversed the empty egg-shell on top of them. This little operation concluded, he smiled on the neat effect, and then beamed affectionately on us both.

'Come, my friends, you are men of intelligence. Ask yourself the question I asked myself. "If I were this man, where should *I* hide?" Hastings, what do you say?'

'Well,' I said, 'I'm rather inclined to think I'd not do a bolt at all. I'd stay in London – in the heart of things, travel by tubes and buses; ten to one I'd never be recognized. There's safety in a crowd.'

Poirot turned inquiringly to Japp.

'I don't agree. Get clear away at once – that's the only chance. I would have had plenty of time to prepare things beforehand. I'd have a yacht waiting, with steam up, and I'd be off to one of the most out-of-the-way corners of the world before the hue and cry began!'

We both looked at Poirot. 'What do *you* say, monsieur?'

For a moment he remained silent. Then a very curious smile flitted across his face.

'My friends, if *I* were hiding from the police, do you know *where* I should hide? *In a prison!*'

'*What?*'

'You are seeking Monsieur Davenheim in order to put him in prison, so you never dream of looking to see if he may not be already there!'

'What do you mean?'

'You tell me Madame Davenheim is not a very intelligent woman. Nevertheless I think if you took her up to Bow Street and confronted her with the man Billy Kellett she would recognize him! In spite of the fact that he has shaved his beard and moustache and those bushy eyebrows, and has cropped his hair close. A woman nearly always knows her husband, though the rest of the world may be deceived.'

'Billy Kellett? But he's known to the police!'

'Did I not tell you Davenheim was a clever man? He prepared his alibi long beforehand. He was not in Buenos Aires last autumn – he was creating the character of Billy Kellett, "doing three months", so that the police should have no suspicions when the time came. He was playing, remember, for a large fortune, as well as liberty. It was worth while doing the thing thoroughly. Only –'

'Yes?'

'*Eh bien*, afterwards he had to wear a false beard and wig, had to *make up as himself again*, and to sleep with a false beard is not easy – it invites detection! He cannot risk continuing to share the chamber of madame his wife. You found out for me that for the last six months, or ever since his supposed return from Buenos Aires, he and Mrs Davenheim occupied separate rooms. Then I was sure! Everything fitted in. The gardener who fancied he saw his master going round to the side of the house was quite right. He went to the boathouse, donned his "tramp" clothes, which you may be sure had been safely hidden from the eyes of his valet, dropped the others in the lake, and proceeded to carry out his plan by pawning the ring in an obvious manner, and then assaulting a policeman, getting himself safely into the haven of Bow Street, where nobody would ever dream of looking for him!'

'It's impossible,' murmured Japp.

'Ask Madame,' said my friend, smiling.

The next day a registered letter lay beside Poirot's plate. He opened it and a five-pound note fluttered out. My friend's brow puckered.

'*Ah, sacré!* But what shall I do with it? I have much remorse! *Ce pauvre Japp?* Ah, an idea! We will have a little dinner, we three! That consoles me. It was really too easy. I am ashamed. I, who would not rob a child – *mille tonnerres! Mon ami*, what have you, that you laugh so heartily?'

Part 10

The Adventure of the Italian Nobleman

Poirot and I had many friends and acquaintances of an informal nature. Amongst these was to be numbered Dr Hawker, a near neighbour of ours, and a member of the medical profession. It was the genial doctor's habit to drop in sometimes of an evening and have a chat with Poirot, of whose genius he was an ardent admirer. The doctor himself, frank and unsuspicious to the last degree, admired the talents so far removed from his own.

On one particular evening in early June, he arrived about half past eight and settled down to a comfortable discussion on the cheery topic of the prevalence of arsenical poisoning in crimes. It must have been about a quarter of an hour later when the door of our sitting room flew open, and a distracted female precipitated herself into the room.

'Oh, doctor, you're wanted! Such a terrible voice. It gave me a turn, it did indeed.'

I recognized in our new visitor Dr Hawker's house-keeper, Miss Rider. The doctor was a bachelor, and lived in a gloomy old house a few streets away. The usually placid Miss Rider was now in a state bordering on incoherence.

'What terrible voice? Who is it, and what's the trouble?'

'It was the telephone, doctor. I answered it – and a voice spoke. "Help," it said. "Doctor – help. They've killed me!" Then it sort of tailed away. "Who's speaking?" I said. "Who's speaking?" Then I got a reply, just a whisper, it seemed, "Foscatine" – something like that – "Regent's Court".'

The doctor uttered an exclamation.

'Count Foscatini. He has a flat in Regent's Court. I must go at once. What can have happened?'

'A patient of yours?' asked Poirot.

'I attended him for some slight ailment a few weeks ago. An Italian, but he speaks English perfectly. Well, I must wish you good night, Monsieur Poirot, unless –' He hesitated.

'I perceive the thought in your mind,' said Poirot, smiling. 'I shall be delighted to accompany you. Hastings, run down and get hold of a taxi.'

Taxis always make themselves sought for when one is particularly pressed for time, but I captured one at last, and we were soon bowling along in the direction of

Regent's Park. Regent's Court was a new block of flats, situated just off St John's Wood Road. They had only recently been built, and contained the latest service devices.

There was no one in the hall. The doctor pressed the lift-bell impatiently, and when the lift arrived questioned the uniformed attendant sharply.

'Flat 11. Count Foscatini. There's been an accident there, I understand.'

The man stared at him.

'First I've heard of it. Mr Graves – that's Count Foscatini's man – went out about half an hour ago, and he said nothing.'

'Is the Count alone in the flat?'

'No, sir, he's got two gentlemen dining with him.'

'What are they like?' I asked eagerly.

We were in the lift now, ascending rapidly to the second floor, on which Flat 11 was situated.

'I didn't see them myself, sir, but I understand that they were foreign gentlemen.'

He pulled back the iron door, and we stepped out on the landing. No 11 was opposite to us. The doctor rang the bell. There was no reply, and we could hear no sound from within. The doctor rang again and again; we could hear the bell trilling within, but no sign of life rewarded us.

'This is getting serious,' muttered the doctor. He turned to the lift attendant.

Agatha Christie

'Is there any pass-key to this door?'

'There is one in the porter's office downstairs.'

'Get it, then, and, look here, I think you'd better send for the police.'

Poirot approved with a nod of the head.

The man returned shortly; with him came the manager.

'Will you tell me, gentlemen, what is the meaning of all this?'

'Certainly. I received a telephone message from Count Foscatini stating that he had been attacked and was dying. You can understand that we must lose no time – if we are not already too late.'

The manager produced the key without more ado, and we all entered the flat.

We passed first into the small square lounge hall. A door on the right of it was half open. The manager indicated it with a nod.

'The dining room.'

Dr Hawker led the way. We followed close on his heels. As we entered the room I gave a gasp. The round table in the centre bore the remains of a meal; three chairs were pushed back, as though their occupants had just risen. In the corner, to the right of the fireplace, was a big writing-table, and sitting at it was a man – or what had been a man. His right hand still grasped the base of the telephone, but he had fallen forward, struck down by a terrific blow on the head from behind. The weapon was not far to seek. A marble statue stood where it had been hurriedly put down, the base of it stained with blood.

The doctor's examination did not take a minute. 'Stone dead. Must have been almost instantaneous. I wonder he even managed to telephone. It will be better not to move him until the police arrive.'

On the manager's suggestion we searched the flat, but the result was a foregone conclusion. It was not likely that the murderers would be concealed there when all they had to do was to walk out.

We came back to the dining room. Poirot had not accompanied us in our tour. I found him studying the centre table with close attention. I joined him. It was a well-polished round mahogany table. A bowl of roses decorated the centre, and white lace mats reposed on the gleaming surface. There was a dish of fruit, but the three dessert plates were untouched. There were three coffee-cups with remains of coffee in them – two black, one with milk. All three men had taken port, and the decanter, half-full, stood before the centre plate. One of the men had smoked a cigar, the other two cigarettes. A tortoiseshell-and-silver box, holding cigars and cigarettes, stood open upon the table.

I enumerated all these facts to myself, but I was forced to admit that they did not shed any brilliant light on the situation. I wondered what Poirot saw in them to make him so intent. I asked him.

'*Mon ami*,' he replied, 'you miss the point. I am looking for something that I do *not* see.'

'What is that?'

'A mistake – even a little mistake – on the part of the murderer.'

He stepped swiftly to the small adjoining kitchen, looked in, and shook his head.

'Monsieur,' he said to the manager, 'explain to me, I pray, your system of serving meals here.'

The manager stepped to a small hatch in the wall.

'This is the service lift,' he explained. 'It runs to the kitchens at the top of the building. You order through this telephone, and the dishes are sent down in the lift, one course at a time. The dirty plates and dishes are sent up in the same manner. No domestic worries, you understand, and at the same time you avoid the wearying publicity of always dining in a restaurant.'

Poirot nodded.

'Then the plates and dishes that were used tonight are on high in the kitchen. You permit that I mount there?'

'Oh, certainly, if you like! Roberts, the lift man, will take you up and introduce you; but I'm afraid you won't find anything that's of any use. They're handling hundreds of plates and dishes, and they'll be all lumped together.'

Poirot remained firm, however, and together we visited the kitchens and questioned the man who had taken the order from Flat 11.

'The order was given from the à la carte menu – for three,' he explained. 'Soup julienne, filet de sole normande, tournedos of beef, and a rice soufflé. What time? Just about eight o'clock, I should say. No, I'm afraid the plates and dishes have been all washed up by now. Unfortunate. You were thinking of fingerprints, I suppose?'

'Not exactly,' said Poirot, with an enigmatical smile. 'I am more interested in Count Foscatini's appetite. Did he partake of every dish?'

'Yes; but of course I can't say how much of each he ate. The plates were all soiled, and the dishes empty – that is to say, with the exception of the rice soufflé. There was a fair amount of that left.'

'Ah!' said Poirot, and seemed satisfied with the fact.

As we descended to the flat again he remarked in a low tone:

'We have decidedly to do with a man of method.'

'Do you mean the murderer, or Count Foscatini?'

'The latter was undoubtedly an orderly gentleman. After imploring help and announcing his approaching demise, he carefully hung up the telephone receiver.'

I stared at Poirot. His words now and his recent inquiries gave me the glimmering of an idea.

'You suspect poison?' I breathed. 'The blow on the head was a blind.'

Poirot merely smiled.

We re-entered the flat to find the local inspector of police had arrived with two constables. He was inclined to resent our appearance, but Poirot calmed him with the mention of our Scotland Yard friend, Inspector Japp, and we were accorded a grudging permission to remain. It was a lucky thing we were, for we had not been back five minutes before an agitated middle-aged man came rushing into the room with every appearance of grief and agitation.

This was Graves, valet-butler to the late Count Foscatini. The story he had to tell was a sensational one.

On the previous morning, two gentlemen had called to see his master. They were Italians, and the elder of the two, a man of about forty, gave his name as Signor Ascanio. The younger was a well-dressed lad of about twenty-four.

Count Foscatini was evidently prepared for their visit and immediately sent Graves out upon some trivial errand. Here the man paused and hesitated in his story. In the end, however, he admitted that, curious as to the purport of the interview, he had not obeyed immediately, but had lingered about endeavouring to hear something of what was going on.

The conversation was carried on in so low a tone that he was not as successful as he had hoped; but he gathered enough to make it clear that some kind of monetary proposition was being discussed, and that the basis of it was a threat. The discussion was anything but amicable. In the end, Count Foscatini raised his voice slightly, and the listener heard these words clearly:

'I have no time to argue further now, gentlemen. If you will dine with me tomorrow night at eight o'clock, we will resume the discussion.'

Afraid of being discovered listening, Graves had then hurried out to do his master's errand. This evening the two men had arrived punctually at eight. During dinner they had talked of indifferent matters – politics, the weather, and the theatrical world. When Graves had placed the port upon the table and brought in the coffee his master told him that he might have the evening off.

'Was that a usual proceeding of his when he had guests?' asked the inspector.

'No, sir; it wasn't. That's what made me think it

must be some business of a very unusual kind that he was going to discuss with these gentlemen.'

That finished Graves's story. He had gone out about 8.30, and meeting a friend, had accompanied him to the Metropolitan Music Hall in Edgware Road.

Nobody had seen the two men leave, but the time of the murder was fixed clearly enough at 8.47. A small clock on the writing-table had been swept off by Foscatini's arm, and had stopped at that hour, which agreed with Miss Rider's telephone summons.

The police surgeon had made his examination of the body, and it was now lying on the couch. I saw the face for the first time – the olive complexion, the long nose, the luxuriant black moustache, and the full red lips drawn back from the dazzlingly white teeth. Not altogether a pleasant face.

'Well,' said the inspector, refastening his notebook. 'The case seems clear enough. The only difficulty will be to lay our hands on this Signor Ascanio. I suppose his address is not in the dead man's pocket-book by any chance?'

As Poirot had said, the late Foscatini was an orderly man. Neatly written in small, precise handwriting was the inscription, 'Signor Paolo Ascanio, Grosvenor Hotel.'

The inspector busied himself with the telephone, then turned to us with a grin.

'Just in time. Our fine gentleman was off to catch the boat train to the Continent. Well, gentlemen, that's about all we can do here. It's a bad business, but straightforward enough. One of these Italian vendetta things, as likely as not.'

Thus airily dismissed, we found our way downstairs. Dr Hawker was full of excitement.

'Like the beginning of a novel, eh? Real exciting stuff. Wouldn't believe it if you read about it.'

Poirot did not speak. He was very thoughtful. All the evening he had hardly opened his lips.

'What says the master detective, eh?' asked Hawker, clapping him on the back. 'Nothing to work your grey cells over this time.'

'You think not?'

'What could there be?'

'Well, for example, there is the window.'

'The window? But it was fastened. Nobody could have got out or in that way. I noticed it specially.'

'And why were you able to notice it?'

The doctor looked puzzled. Poirot hastened to explain.

'It is to the curtains that I refer. They were not drawn. A little odd, that. And then there was the coffee. It was very black coffee.'

'Well, what of it?'

'Very black,' repeated Poirot. 'In conjunction with

that let us remember that very little of the rice soufflé was eaten, and we get – what?'

'Moonshine,' laughed the doctor. 'You're pulling my leg.'

'Never do I pull the leg. Hastings here knows that I am perfectly serious.'

'I don't know what you are getting at, all the same,' I confessed. 'You don't suspect the manservant, do you? He might have been in with the gang, and put some dope in the coffee. I suppose they'll test his alibi?'

'Without doubt, my friend; but it is the alibi of Signor Ascanio that interests me.'

'You think he has an alibi?'

'That is just what worries me. I have no doubt that we shall soon be enlightened on that point.'

The *Daily Newsmonger* enabled us to become conversant with succeeding events.

Signor Ascanio was arrested and charged with the murder of Count Foscatini. When arrested, he denied knowing the Count, and declared he had never been near Regent's Court either on the evening of the crime or on the previous morning. The younger man had disappeared entirely. Signor Ascanio had arrived alone at the Grosvenor Hotel from the Continent two days before the murder. All efforts to trace the second man failed.

Ascanio, however, was not sent for trial. No less a

personage than the Italian Ambassador himself came forward and testified at the police-court proceedings that Ascanio had been with him at the Embassy from eight till nine that evening. The prisoner was discharged. Naturally, a lot of people thought that the crime was a political one, and was being deliberately hushed up.

Poirot had taken a keen interest in all these points. Nevertheless, I was somewhat surprised when he suddenly informed me one morning that he was expecting a visitor at eleven o'clock, and that the visitor was none other than Ascanio himself.

'He wishes to consult you?'

'*Du tout*, Hastings, I wish to consult him.'

'What about?'

'The Regent's Court murder.'

'You are going to prove that he did it?'

'A man cannot be tried twice for murder, Hastings. Endeavour to have the common sense. Ah, that is our friend's ring.'

A few minutes later Signor Ascanio was ushered in – a small, thin man with a secretive and furtive glance in his eyes. He remained standing, darting suspicious glances from one to the other of us.

'Monsieur Poirot?'

My little friend tapped himself gently on the chest. 'Be seated, signor. You received my note. I am determined to get to the bottom of this mystery. In some small measure you can aid me. Let us commence. You – in company with a friend – visited the late Count Foscatini on the morning of Tuesday the 9th –'

The Italian made an angry gesture.

'I did nothing of the sort. I have sworn in court –'

'*Précisément* – and I have a little idea that you have sworn falsely.'

'You threaten me? Bah! I have nothing to fear from you. I have been acquitted.'

'Exactly; and as I am not an imbecile, it is not with the gallows I threaten you – but with publicity. Publicity! I see that you do not like the word. I had an idea that you would not. My little ideas, you know, they are very valuable to me. Come, signor, your only chance is to be frank with me. I do not ask to know whose indiscretions brought you to England. I know this much, you came for the special purpose of seeing Count Foscatini.'

'He was not a count,' growled the Italian.

'I have already noted the fact that his name does not appear in the *Almanach de Gotha*. Never mind, the title of count is often useful in the profession of blackmailing.'

'I suppose I might as well be frank. You seem to know a good deal.'

'I have employed my grey cells to some advantage.

Come, Signor Ascanio, you visited the dead man on the Tuesday morning – that is so, is it not?'

'Yes; but I never went there on the following evening. There was no need. I will tell you all. Certain information concerning a man of great position in Italy had come into this scoundrel's possession. He demanded a big sum of money in return for the papers. I came over to England to arrange the matter. I called upon him by appointment that morning. One of the young secretaries of the Embassy was with me. The Count was more reasonable than I had hoped, although even then the sum of money I paid him was a huge one.'

'Pardon, how was it paid?'

'In Italian notes of comparatively small denomination. I paid over the money then and there. He handed me the incriminating papers. I never saw him again.'

'Why did you not say all this when you were arrested?'

'In my delicate position I was forced to deny any association with the man.'

'And how do you account for the events of the evening then?'

'I can only think that someone must have deliberately impersonated me. I understand that no money was found in the flat.'

Poirot looked at him and shook his head.

'Strange,' he murmured. 'We all have the little grey

cells. And so few of us know how to use them. Good morning, Signor Ascanio. I believe your story. It is very much as I had imagined. But I had to make sure.'

After bowing his guest out, Poirot returned to his armchair and smiled at me.

'Let us hear M. le Capitaine Hastings on the case.'

'Well, I suppose Ascanio is right – somebody impersonated him.'

'Never, never will you use the brains the good God has given you. Recall to yourself some words I uttered after leaving the flat that night. I referred to the window-curtains not being drawn. We are in the month of June. It is still light at eight o'clock. The light is failing by half-past. *Ça vous dit quelque chose?* I perceive a struggling impression that you will arrive some day. Now let us continue. The coffee was, as I said, very black. Count Foscatini's teeth were magnificently white. Coffee stains the teeth. We reason from that that Count Foscatini did not drink any coffee. Yet there was coffee in all three cups. Why should anyone pretend Count Foscatini had drunk coffee when he had not done so?'

I shook my head, utterly bewildered.

'Come, I will help you. What evidence have we that Ascanio and his friend, or two men posing as them, ever came to the flat that night? Nobody saw them go in; nobody saw them go out. We have the evidence of one man and of a host of inanimate objects.'

'You mean?'

'I mean knives and forks and plates and empty dishes. Ah, but it was a clever idea! Graves is a thief and a scoundrel, but what a man of method! He overhears a portion of the conversation in the morning, enough to realize that Ascanio will be in an awkward position to defend himself. The following evening, about eight o'clock, he tells his master he is wanted at the telephone. Foscatini sits down, stretches out his hand to the telephone, and from behind Graves strikes him down with the marble figure. Then quickly to the service telephone – dinner for three! It comes, he lays the table, dirties the plates, knives, and forks, etc. But he has to get rid of the food too. Not only is he a man of brain; he has a resolute and capacious stomach! But after eating three tournedos, the rice soufflé is too much for him! He even smokes a cigar and two cigarettes to carry out the illusion. Ah, but it was magnificently thorough! Then, having moved on the hands of the clock to 8.47, he smashes it and stops it. The one thing he does not do is to draw the curtains. But if there had been a real dinner party the curtains would have been drawn as soon as the light began to fail. Then he hurries out, mentioning the guests to the lift man in passing. He hurries to a telephone box, and as near as possible to

8.47 rings up the doctor with his master's dying cry. So successful is his idea that no one ever inquires if a call was put through from Flat 11 at that time.'

'Except Hercule Poirot, I suppose?' I said sarcastically.

'Not even Hercule Poirot,' said my friend, with a smile. 'I am about to inquire now. I had to prove my point to you first. But you will see, I shall be right; and then Japp, to whom I have already given a hint, will be able to arrest the respectable Graves. I wonder how much of the money he has spent.'

Poirot *was* right. He always is, confound him!

Part 11

The Case of the Missing Will

The problem presented to us by Miss Violet Marsh made rather a pleasant change from our usual routine work. Poirot had received a brisk and businesslike note from the lady asking for an appointment, and had replied asking her to call upon him at eleven o'clock the following day.

She arrived punctually – a tall, handsome young woman, plainly but neatly dressed, with an assured and businesslike manner. Clearly a young woman who meant to get on in the world. I am not a great admirer of the so-called New Woman myself, and, in spite of her good looks, I was not particularly prepossessed in her favour.

'My business is of a somewhat unusual nature, Monsieur Poirot,' she began, after she had accepted a chair. 'I had better begin at the beginning and tell you the whole story.'

'If you please, mademoiselle.'

'I am an orphan. My father was one of two brothers, sons of a small yeoman farmer in Devonshire. The farm was a poor one, and the elder brother, Andrew, emigrated to Australia, where he did very well indeed, and by means of successful speculation in land became a very rich man. The younger brother, Roger (my father), had no leanings towards the agricultural life. He managed to educate himself a little, and obtained a post as clerk with a small firm. He married slightly above him; my mother was the daughter of a poor artist. My father died when I was six years old. When I was fourteen, my mother followed him to the grave. My only living relation then was my uncle Andrew, who had recently returned from Australia and bought a small place, Crabtree Manor, in his native county. He was exceedingly kind to his brother's orphan child, took me to live with him, and treated me in every way as though I was his own daughter.

'Crabtree Manor, in spite of its name, is really only an old farmhouse. Farming was in my uncle's blood, and he was intensely interested in various modern farming experiments. Although kindness itself to me, he had certain peculiar and deeply-rooted ideas as to the upbringing of women. Himself a man of little or no education, though possessing remarkable shrewdness, he placed little value on what he called "book knowledge". He was especially opposed to the education of women. In his opinion, girls should learn practical housework and dairy-work, be useful about the home, and have as little to do with book learning as possible. He proposed to bring me up on these lines, to my bitter disappointment and annoyance. I rebelled frankly. I knew that I possessed a good brain, and had absolutely no talent for domestic duties. My uncle and I had many bitter arguments on the subject, for, though much attached to each other, we were both self-willed. I was lucky enough to win a scholarship, and up to a certain point was successful in getting my own way. The crisis arose when I resolved to go to Girton. I had a little money of my own, left me by my mother, and I was quite determined to make the best use of the gifts God had given me. I had one long, final argument with my uncle. He put the facts plainly before me. He had no other relations, and he had intended me to be his sole heiress. As I have told you, he was a very rich man. If I persisted in these "new-fangled notions" of mine, however, I need look for nothing from him. I remained polite, but firm. I should always be deeply attached to him, I told him, but I must lead my own life. We parted on that note. "You fancy your brains, my girl," were his last words. "I've no book learning, but, for all that, I'll pit mine against yours any day. We'll see what we shall see.""

'That was nine years ago. I have stayed with him for a weekend occasionally, and our relations were perfectly amicable, though his views remained unaltered. He never referred to my having matriculated, nor to my BSc. For the last three years his health had been failing, and a month ago he died.

'I am now coming to the point of my visit. My uncle left a most extraordinary will. By its terms, Crabtree Manor and its contents are to be at my disposal for a year from his death – "during which time my clever niece may prove her wits", the actual words run. At the end of that period, "my wits having been proved better than hers", the house and all my uncle's large fortune pass to various charitable institutions.'

'That is a little hard on you, mademoiselle, seeing that you were Mr Marsh's only blood relation.'

'I do not look on it in that way. Uncle Andrew warned me fairly, and I chose my own path. Since I would not fall in with his wishes, he was at perfect liberty to leave his money to whom he pleased.'

'Was the will drawn up by a lawyer?'

'No; it was written on a printed will-form and witnessed by the man and his wife who live at the house and do for my uncle.'

'There might be a possibility of upsetting such a will?'

'I would not even attempt to do such a thing.'

'You regard it then as a sporting challenge on the part of your uncle?'

'That is exactly how I look upon it.'

'It bears that interpretation, certainly,' said Poirot thoughtfully. 'Somewhere in this rambling old manor-house your uncle has concealed either a sum of money in notes or possibly a second will, and has given you a year in which to exercise your ingenuity to find it.'

'Exactly, Monsieur Poirot; and I am paying you the compliment of assuming that your ingenuity will be greater than mine.'

'Eh, eh! but that is very charming of you. My grey cells are at your disposal. You have made no search yourself?'

'Only a cursory one; but I have too much respect for my uncle's undoubted abilities to fancy that the task will be an easy one.'

'Have you the will or a copy of it with you?'

Miss March handed a document across the table. Poirot ran through it, nodding to himself.

'Made three years ago. Dated March 25; and the time is given also – 11 A.M. – that is very suggestive. It narrows the field of search. Assuredly it is another will we have to seek for. A will made even half an hour later would upset this. *Eh bien*, mademoiselle, it is a problem charming and ingenious that you have presented to me here. I shall have all the pleasure in the world in solving it for you. Granted that your uncle was a man of ability, his grey cells cannot have been of the quality of Hercule Poirot's!'

(Really, Poirot's vanity is blatant!)

'Fortunately, I have nothing of moment on hand at the minute. Hastings and I will go down to Crabtree Manor tonight. The man and wife who attended on your uncle are still there, I presume?'

'Yes, their name is Baker.'

II

The following morning saw us started on the hunt proper. We had arrived late the night before. Mr and Mrs Baker, having received a telegram from Miss Marsh, were expecting us. They were a pleasant couple, the man gnarled and pink-cheeked, like a shrivelled pippin, and his wife a woman of vast proportion and true Devonshire calm.

Tired with our journey and the eight-mile drive from the station, we had retired at once to bed after a supper of roast chicken, apple pie, and Devonshire cream. We had now disposed of an excellent breakfast, and were sitting in a small panelled room which had been the late Mr Marsh's study and living room. A roll-top desk stuffed with papers, all neatly docketed, stood against the wall, and a big leather armchair showed plainly that it had been its owner's constant resting-place. A big chintz-covered settee ran along the opposite wall, and the deep low window seats were covered with the same faded chintz of an old-fashioned pattern.

'*Eh bien, mon ami,*' said Poirot, lighting one of his tiny cigarettes, 'we must map out our plan of campaign. Already I have made a rough survey of the house, but I am of the opinion that any clue will be found in this room. We shall have to go through the documents in the desk with meticulous care. Naturally, I do not expect to find the will amongst them, but it is likely that some apparently innocent paper may conceal the clue to its hiding-place. But first we must have a little information. Ring the bell, I pray of you.'

I did so. While we were waiting for it to be answered, Poirot walked up and down, looking about him approvingly.

'A man of method, this Mr Marsh. See how neatly the packets of papers are docketed; then the key to each drawer has its ivory label – so has the key of the china cabinet on the wall; and see with what precision the china within is arranged. It rejoices the heart. Nothing here offends the eye –'

He came to an abrupt pause, as his eye was caught by the key of the desk itself, to which a dirty envelope was affixed. Poirot frowned at it and withdrew it from the lock. On it were scrawled the words: 'Key of Roll Top Desk,' in a crabbed handwriting, quite unlike the neat superscriptions on the other keys.

'An alien note,' said Poirot, frowning. 'I could swear that here we have no longer the personality of Mr Marsh. But who else has been in the house? Only Miss Marsh, and she, if I mistake not, is also a young lady of method and order.'

Baker came in answer to the bell.

'Will you fetch madame your wife, and answer a few questions?'

Baker departed, and in a few moments returned with Mrs Baker, wiping her hands on her apron and beaming all over her face.

In a few clear words Poirot set forth the object of his mission. The Bakers were immediately sympathetic.

'Us don't want to see Miss Violet done out of what's hers,' declared the woman. 'Cruel hard 'twould be for hospitals to get it all.'

Poirot proceeded with his questions. Yes, Mr and Mrs Baker remembered perfectly witnessing the will. Baker had previously been sent into the neighbouring town to get two printed will-forms.

'Two?' said Poirot sharply.

'Yes, sir, for safety like, I suppose, in case he should spoil one – and sure enough, so he did do. Us had signed one –'

'What time of day was that?'

Baker scratched his head, but his wife was quicker.

'Why, to be sure, I'd just put the milk on for the cocoa at eleven. Don't ee remember? It had all boiled over on the stove when us got back to kitchen.'

'And afterwards?'

''Twould be about an hour later. Us had to go in again. "I've made a mistake," said old master, "had to tear the whole thing up. I'll trouble you to sign again," and us did. And afterwards master gave us a tidy sum of money each. "I've left you nothing in my will," says he, "but each year I live you'll have this to be a nest-egg when I'm gone": and sure enough, so he did.'

Poirot reflected.

'After you had signed the second time, what did Mr Marsh do? Do you know?'

'Went out to the village to pay tradesmen's books.'

That did not seem very promising. Poirot tried another tack. He held out the key of the desk.

'Is that your master's writing?'

I may have imagined it, but I fancied that a moment or two elapsed before Baker replied: 'Yes, sir, it is.'

'He's lying,' I thought. 'But why?'

'Has your master let the house? – have there been any strangers in it during the last three years?'

'No, sir.'

'No visitors?'

'Only Miss Violet.'

'No strangers of any kind been inside this room?'

'No, sir.'

'You forget the workmen, Jim,' his wife reminded him.

'Workmen?' Poirot wheeled round on her. 'What workmen?'

The woman explained that about two years and a half ago workmen had been in the house to do certain repairs. She was quite vague as to what the repairs were. Her view seemed to be that the whole thing was a fad of her master's and quite unnecessary. Part of the time the workmen had been in the study; but what they had done there she could not say, as her master had not let either of them into the room whilst the work was in progress. Unfortunately, they could not remember the name of the firm employed, beyond the fact that it was a Plymouth one.

'We progress, Hastings,' said Poirot, rubbing his hands as the Bakers left the room. 'Clearly he made a second will and then had workmen from Plymouth in to make a suitable hiding-place. Instead of wasting time taking up the floor and tapping the walls, we will go to Plymouth.'

With a little trouble, we were able to get the information we wanted. After one or two essays we found the firm employed by Mr Marsh.

Their employees had all been with them many years, and it was easy to find the two men who had worked under Mr Marsh's orders. They remembered the job perfectly. Amongst various other minor jobs, they had taken up one of the bricks of the old-fashioned fireplace, made a cavity beneath, and so cut the brick that it was impossible to see the join. By pressing on the second brick from the end, the whole thing was raised. It had been quite a complicated piece of work, and the old gentleman had been very fussy about it. Our informant was a man called Coghan, a big, gaunt man with a grizzled moustache. He seemed an intelligent fellow.

We returned to Crabtree Manor in high spirits, and, locking the study door, proceeded to put our newly acquired knowledge into effect. It was impossible to see any sign on the bricks, but when we pressed in the manner indicated, a deep cavity was at once disclosed.

Eagerly Poirot plunged in his hand. Suddenly his face fell from complacent elation to consternation. All he held was a charred fragment of stiff paper. But for it, the cavity was empty.

'*Sacre!*' cried Poirot angrily. 'Someone has been before us.'

We examined the scrap of paper anxiously. Clearly it was a fragment of what we sought. A portion of Baker's

Agatha Christie

signature remained, but no indication of what the terms of the will had been.

Poirot sat back on his heels. His expression would have been comical if we had not been so overcome. 'I understand it not,' he growled. 'Who destroyed this? And what was their object?'

'The Bakers?' I suggested.

'*Pourquoi?* Neither will makes any provision for them, and they are more likely to be kept on with Miss Marsh than if the place became the property of a hospital. How could it be to anyone's advantage to destroy the will? The hospitals benefit – yes; but one cannot suspect institutions.'

'Perhaps the old man changed his mind and destroyed it himself,' I suggested.

Poirot rose to his feet, dusting his knees with his usual care.

'That may be,' he admitted, 'one of your more sensible observations, Hastings. Well, we can do no more here. We have done all that mortal man can do. We have successfully pitted our wits against the late Andrew Marsh's; but, unfortunately, his niece is not better off for our success.'

By driving to the station at once, we were just able to catch a train to London, though not the principal express. Poirot was sad and dissatisfied. For my part, I was tired and dozed in a corner. Suddenly, as we were just moving out of Taunton, Poirot uttered a piercing squeal.

'*Vite*, Hastings! Awake and jump! But jump I say!'

Before I knew where I was we were standing on the platform, bareheaded and minus our valises, whilst the train disappeared into the night. I was furious. But Poirot paid no attention.

'Imbecile that I have been!' he cried. 'Triple imbecile! Not again will I vaunt my little grey cells!'

'That's a good job at any rate,' I said grumpily. 'But what is this all about?'

As usual, when following out his own ideas, Poirot paid absolutely no attention to me.

'The tradesmen's books – I have left them entirely out of account? Yes, but where? Where? Never mind, I cannot be mistaken. We must return at once.'

Easier said than done. We managed to get a slow train to Exeter, and there Poirot hired a car. We arrived back at Crabtree Manor in the small hours of the morning. I pass over the bewilderment of the Bakers when we had at last aroused them. Paying no attention to anybody, Poirot strode at once to the study.

'I have been, not a triple imbecile, but thirty-six times one, my friend,' he deigned to remark. 'Now, behold!'

Going straight to the desk he drew out the key, and detached the envelope from it. I stared at him stupidly.

How could he possibly hope to find a big will-form in that tiny envelope? With great care he cut open the envelope, laying it out flat. Then he lighted the fire and held the plain inside surface of the envelope to the flame. In a few minutes faint characters began to appear.

'Look, *mon ami!*' cried Poirot in triumph.

I looked. There were just a few lines of faint writing stating briefly that he left everything to his niece, Violet Marsh. It was dated March 25 12.30 P.M., and witnessed by Albert Pike, confectioner, and Jessie Pike, married woman.

'But is it legal?' I gasped.

'As far as I know, there is no law against writing your will in a blend of disappearing and sympathetic ink. The intention of the testator is clear, and the beneficiary is his only living relation. But the cleverness of him! He foresaw every step that a searcher would take – that I, miserable imbecile, took. He gets two will-forms, makes the servants sign twice, then sallies out with his will written on the inside of a dirty envelope and a fountain-pen containing his little ink mixture. On some excuse he gets the confectioner and his wife to sign their names under his own signature, then he ties it to the key of his desk and chuckles to himself. If his niece sees through his little ruse, she will have justified her choice of life and elaborate education and be thoroughly welcome to his money.'

'She didn't see through it, did she?' I said slowly. 'It seems rather unfair. The old man really won.'

'But no, Hastings. It is *your* wits that go astray. Miss Marsh proved the astuteness of her wits and the value of the higher education for women by at once putting the matter in *my* hands. Always employ the expert. She has amply proved her right to the money.'

I wonder – I very much wonder – what old Andrew Marsh would have thought!

The Mysterious Affair At Styles

POIROT'S FIRST CASE

Agatha Christie

Peril to the detective who says: "It is so small – it does not matter…" Everything matters.'

When Emily Inglethorpe is found murdered, Captain Hastings calls for help from an old friend: a certain Belgian detective who has grown bored of retirement.

A shattered coffee cup, a splash of candle grease, a bed of begonias – only Poirot could unravel an ingenious crime from these few intriguing clues.

'Almost too ingenious.'   *Times Literary Supplement*

ISBN-13 978-0-00-711927-1

Murder on the Orient Express

POIROT

Agatha Christie

'The murderer is with us – on the train now…'

Just after midnight, the famous *Orient Express* is stopped in its tracks by a snowdrift. By morning, Hercule Poirot knows that the millionaire Simon Ratchett lies dead in his compartment, stabbed a dozen times, his door locked from the inside. One of his fellow passengers must be the murderer.

Isolated by the storm and with a killer in their midst, detective Hercule Poirot must find the killer amongst a dozen of the dead man's enemies, before the murderer decides to strike again…

'Very real, and keeps readers enthralled and guessing to the end.'   *Times Literary Supplement*

ISBN-13 978-0-00-711931-8

The ABC Murders

POIROT

Agatha Christie

'Let us see, Mr Clever Poirot, just how clever you can be.'

There's a serial killer on the loose, working his way through the alphabet, and the whole country is in a state of panic.

A is for Mrs Ascher in Andover, B is for Betty Barnard in Bexhill, C is for Sir Carmichael Clarke in Churston. With each murder, the killer is getting more confident – but leaving a trail of deliberate clues to taunt the proud Hercule Poirot might just prove to be the first, and fatal mistake…

'An entirely original idea.' *Daily Telegraph*

'Christie is to be congratulated on the perfection of her invention.' *The Times*

ISBN-13 978-0-00-711929-5

Five Little Pigs

POIROT

Agatha Christie

Beautiful Caroline Crale was convicted of poisoning her husband, but just like the nursery rhyme, there were five other 'little pigs' who could have done it: Philip Blake (the stockbroker) who went to market; Meredith Blake (the amateur herbalist) who stayed at home; Elsa Greer (the three-time divorcee) who had her roast beef; Cecilia Williams (the devoted governess) who had none; and Angela Warren (the disfigured sister) who cried all the way home.

Sixteen years later, Caroline's daughter is determined to prove her mother's innocence, and Poirot just can't get that nursery rhyme out of his mind...

'Mrs Christie as usual puts a ring through the reader's nose and leads him to one of her smashing last-minute showdowns.'   *Observer*

'The answer to the riddle is brilliant.'
                                    Times Literary Supplement

ISBN-13 978-0-00-712073-4

Lord Edgware Dies

POIROT

Agatha Christie

When Lord Edgware is found murdered the police are baffled. His estranged actress wife was seen to visit him just before his death and Poirot himself heard her brag of her plan to 'get rid' of him.

After all, how could Jane have stabbed Lord Edgware to death in his library at exactly the same time she was seen dining with friends? It's a case that almost proves to be too much for the great Hercule Poirot.

'The whole case is a triumph of Poirot's special qualities.'
Times Literary Supplement

ISBN-13 978-0-00-712074-1

The Hollow

POIROT

Agatha Christie

A far-from-warm welcome greets Hercule Poirot as he
arrives for lunch at Lucy Angkatell's country house. A man
lies dying by the swimming pool, his blood dripping into
the water and his wife stands over him, holding a revolver.

But as Poirot investigates, he begins to realize that beneath
the respectable surface lies a tangle of family secrets and
everyone becomes a suspect.

'A grade-A plot – the best Christie in years.'
San Francisco Chronicle

ISBN-13 978-0-00-712102-1

Evil Under the Sun

POIROT

Agatha Christie

The beautiful bronzed body of Arlena Stuart lay face down on the beach. But strangely, there was no sun and Arlena was not sun-bathing… she had been strangled.

Ever since Arlena's arrival the air had been thick with sexual tension. Each of the guests had a motive to kill her, including Arlena's new husband, but Hercule Poirot suspects that this apparent 'crime of passion' conceals something more evil and pre-meditated altogether.

'She springs her secret like a land mine.'

Times Literary Supplement

ISBN-13 978-0-00-711926-4